MISSION AT MIDNIGHT

Chronicles of the Westbrook Brides, Book 2

A Sweet Regency Historical Romance

COLLETTE CAMERON

***Blue Rose Romance*®**
Sweet-to-Spicy Timeless Romance®

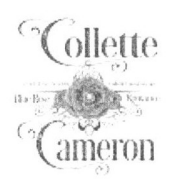

MISSION AT MIDNIGHT
Chronicles of the Westbrook Brides
A Sweet Regency Historical Romance
Copyright © 2023 Collette Cameron®
Cover Art: Angela Horner - Long Valley Designs LLC

All Rights Reserved
This book is a work of fiction. Names, characters, places, and incidents are the product of the author's imagination or are used fictitiously. Any resemblance to actual events, locales, or persons, living or dead, is coincidental.

All rights reserved under International and Pan-American Copyright Conventions. By downloading or purchasing a print copy of this book, you have been granted the *non*-exclusive, *non*-transferable right to access and read the text of this book. No part of this text may be reproduced, transmitted, downloaded, decompiled, reverse engineered, or stored in or introduced into any information storage and retrieval system, in any form or by any means, whether electronic or mechanical, now known or hereinafter invented without the express written permission of the copyright owner.

For permission requests, write to the publisher at the address below.
Attn: Permissions Coordinator
Blue Rose Romance®
PO Box 167
Scappoose, Oregon 97203
collettecameron.com

eBook ISBN: 9781955259408
Print Book ISBN: 9781955259415

Dedication

For everyone who has ever felt out of place and like they don't fit in.

Life is short, break the rules.
Forgive quickly. Kiss slowly.
Love truly. Laugh uncontrollably.
And never regret ANYTHING that makes you smile.
~Mark Twain

Acknowledgements

The stunning cover for *Mission at Midnight* is the artful work of Angela Horner of Long Valley Designs. It leaves me breathless every time I look at it.

Several of my VIP readers in Collette's Cheris offered input about Clodovea's jewelry, the farmhouse, and other details that made the story personal and multifaceted. A special thank you to Janice King for helping me select one of Lucius's middle names.

Other Collette Cameron Books

Chronicles of the Westbrook Brides

Midnight Christmas Waltz

Mission at Midnight

Coming Soon

The Midnight Marquess

Minuet at Midnight

Moonlight Wishes & Midnight Kisses

Holly, Mistletoe, & Midnight Snow

Wishing Upon a Midnight Star

Kiss a Rake at Midnight

Unmasked at Midnight

Once Upon a Midnight Dream

The Wallflower's Midnight Waltz

Memories Made at Midnight

Check out Collette's Other Series

Daughters of Desire

Highland Heather Romancing a Scot

The Culpepper Misses

Heart of a Scot

Castle Brides

Seductive Scoundrels

The Honorable Rogues®

Collections

Lords in Love

Heart of a Scot Books 1-3

The Honorable Rogues® Books 1-3

The Honorable Rogues® Books 4-6

Seductive Scoundrels Series Books 1-3

Seductive Scoundrels Series Books 4-6

The Culpepper Misses Series Books 1-2

Daughters of Desire (Scandalous Ladies) Series Books 1-2

Highland Heather Romancing a Scot Series Books 1-2

1

17 February 1826
Spanish ambassador's home
Regent's Park – London, England
Nearly midnight

Now. Go now. Escape.

As the animated crowd surged toward the grand room in anticipation of the sumptuous supper laid out for Ambassador Domingo Felix Tur de Montis's three hundred and fifty guests, Clodovea seized the opportunity she'd waited nearly three hours to come to pass.

As diligent and protective as her older brothers and dragon-like duenna were, she'd likely not have another chance to escape this god-awful costume ball. Clodovea needed a few moments alone in a quiet place to regain her equanimity and allow her ire to abate.

Not just ire but fulminating hurt and humiliation too.

A fresh wave of mortification engulfed her, and her vision blurred.

No. I shall not cry.

Do not give them the gratification, Clodovea Madeleine Cayetana de Soverosa.

Your father was a noble.

You have noble blood in your veins.

You are not inferior to those women.

Jaw clenched tight, Clodovea blinked away the moisture pooling in her eyes.

She had not let the heartless harridans see her weep at their cruel barbs in the ballroom or retiring room, and she would not give them the victory now. Their cold cat-like eyes had shone with glee behind their elaborate masks as they curved their rouged mouths into satisfied feline smiles.

Why must the lovely English ladies in their clever costumes be so vicious?

Slender, graceful, sophisticated women who enjoyed degrading her for reasons Clodovea could not comprehend. Making a May game of her accent, her costume choice, her struggle with British customs, and her faulty English.

English.

Such an ugly, harsh, unromantic language, unlike the dulcet, warm tones of *la lengua española*.

Snapping her hand-painted ebony lace fan shut while simultaneously grasping the skirts of her black and silver gown in her other hand, she tore down the corridor.

She should never have indulged in the whimsical costume.

Black swan, indeed.

Swans were graceful, elegant creatures.

Clodovea was not.

She more closely resembled a *cara blanca*—a white-faced black Spanish chicken—some of the largest chickens alive. And the fact that she knew such an insignificant detail said much about her and the trite trivia she easily retained.

Thanks to her voluptuous mother—in truth, all her maternal female relations—Clodovea boasted an overly rounded bosom and generous hips. Mama's figure had been alluring, sensual, and oh so feminine, her movements as agile and graceful as a gazelle's.

Not so Clodovea's.

As much as it grieved her, she was…

Plump as a partridge and *plodding as a plow horse. Clodovea the clodpoll.*

A few of the hateful sotto voce whispers directed toward her this evening replayed in her ears.

Never mind that her name was pronounced clode-oh-vee, not clod-dove-ee-ah.

Mama had named her after a mythical warrior, claiming that with three older brothers, she'd need to be strong and courageous.

However, Clodovea wasn't the least warrior-like—not daring or brave or valiant.

Neither was she as stout or clumsy as the stick-thin, shapeless, and flat-chested English ladies inferred.

Nevertheless, she did occasionally tread upon her dance partner's toes and found stays a nuisance beneath her gowns. The undergarment emphasized her cleavage, which needed no enhancement whatsoever and only served to lure lecherous male gazes.

Casting a swift glance behind her, Clodovea released the air she held in her lungs with a trembling sigh.

So far, so good.

She'd even avoided the Spanish guards making their rounds.

At these events, sentinels always patrolled inside and out—though no one openly admitted the gatherings were as much about politics and favors, extortion and exploitation, as entertainment and enjoyment.

Andrés, her oldest brother and a Spanish attaché, had dragged her to these elite assemblies since she'd turned eighteen, six years ago. Clodovea supposed she ought to appreciate the luxury and esteemed company.

Regardless, the truth was that ever since her parents died at a fiesta, she loathed crowds—particularly throngs of people whose high opinions of themselves, elevated noses, and contemptuous glances made her feel like a toad.

An ugly, mud-colored, warty toad.

She dashed along, grateful her lovely beaded silver silk slippers merely pattered—a soft *swish, swish*—on the cold, hard Calacatta gold Italian marble floor rather than clacked loudly with each swift step.

Gazing at herself in the cheval mirror this evening

before leaving their rented Bedford Square house, she'd studied the young woman staring back at her.

Unexceptional but not homely.

Her wavy cocoa-bean-brown hair—her best feature—shone. Confident she'd picked the perfect costume to flatter her buxom figure, a glint of eagerness had lit her almond-shaped hazel eyes.

Tonto. Fool.

The black ostrich feathers tucked into Clodovea's intricate coiffeur frantically wobbled as she sped along, and she fretted they might fall out. Her silver fillagree earrings, set with jet and diamonds, swung back and forth, back and forth, pendulum-like as the jet swan cameo pendant that had belonged to her beautiful, blonde Castilian mother bobbed between her breasts.

A longcase clock somewhere in the house began to chime the midnight hour.

Hurry. Hurry.

You mustn't get caught.

Clodovea had a mission; she must find a hiding place—to recover and re-erect her battlements. So that when she returned to the ball, she could face the rest of the evening composed and with her head held high.

Heart racing, temples pounding, and stupid, *estúpida* stubborn tears still stinging her eyes, she rushed onward, leaving the cacophony of laughing and chatting guests behind.

She rounded a corner, then another, before daring to slow her pace.

Possessing an excellent sense of direction, Clodovea had no concern that she'd lose her way in the great house. With a swift side-eyed glance up and down the passageway, she slipped inside the nearest room, praying no one lingered inside.

If the chamber was occupied, she meant to fib and claim she'd become turned around when returning from the ladies' retiring room.

Two floors above and in the other wing.

If she averted her gaze, hunched her shoulders, and spoke halting English, she might actually get away with the ridiculous lie.

A swift examination of the dim interior brought an involuntary sigh of relief.

Empty.

A low fire burned in the hearth to dispel the permeating February chill.

How Clodovea missed the warmth of her homeland.

Outside, rain and snow wrestled for dominance, and the wind blew the precipitation about with the vengeance of a cross maid shaking a dirty carpet. Hopefully, no dutiful servant would come along to stoke the fire and discover her where she ought not be.

In her desperation to flee, she hadn't considered the repercussions should that occur.

Slowly, her full skirts whooshing softly with the movement, she pivoted, taking in the chamber she'd entered a few seconds ago. It was either a private salon or drawing room and every bit as garishly overdone and elaborate as the rest of the mansion.

A diminutive little man at least five inches shorter than her, the ambassador was a puffed-up braggart.

Nonetheless, the room provided a perfect sanctuary for the next hour.

She'd meant to skip supper tonight, in any event.

To her three older brothers' immense frustration

and the irritation of Lupita Balasco, her nurse turned duenna, Clodovea had begun a reducing diet a fortnight ago.

She slipped the silk strap of her fan around her wrist as she wandered to a settee. As she bent to sink onto the gold and crimson brocade cushion, giggling and rustling echoed outside the door.

Who in the world?

Had someone followed her after all?

Well, she wasn't up to any more abuse at present.

She sprinted across the room and dived behind the draperies.

Clodovea had barely yanked the heavy velvet across the French windows before a couple, locked in a romantic embrace, stumbled into the salon. Heart pounding in her ears and her back pressed against the terrace door handle, she peeked through a half-inch crack. She didn't recognize either person, although something about the woman seemed vaguely familiar.

Giving a throaty, wicked chuckle, the man dressed as a satyr booted the panel shut, locked the door, and then dropped the key in his blood-red jacket pocket.

Clodovea nearly stamped her foot in frustration, but that would reveal her presence.

Por el amor de Dios!

For God's sake.

This couldn't be happening.

The man gave the woman, another Cleopatra—Clodovea had seen at least two other Egyptian queens—a devilish wink.

"No one shall interrupt us, *my* queen."

"Tifton, you are *so* naughty," she replied in a husky purr.

A lover's tryst.

Perfectly wonderful.

Now what was Clodovea to do?

A heartbeat later, the pair collapsed on the second settee and, to Clodovea's horror, began shedding their clothing.

Dios mío!

My God.

Surely, they are not going to…

Sí. Yes.

They were.

MISSION AT MIDNIGHT

It seemed she wasn't the only one using the dinner commotion to sneak away.

Eyes squeezed tight, Clodovea tried to ignore the animalistic sounds, husky moans, and rasping gasps as she fumbled behind her to unlock the door as quietly as possible.

At last, she managed to open the French window, and holding her breath, she sneaked through the opening. Lower lip caught between her teeth, she used both hands to press the panel gently shut.

No guard called for her to halt.

Regardless, one would pass by soon.

She must be away by then.

A gust of wind slammed into Clodovea, and she shivered.

It was a wonder the English didn't have moss and mold growing on them due to the constant dankness and dampness.

While the revelers enjoyed the costume ball, the temperature outside had dropped.

It was freezing, and although the precipitation hadn't ceased completely, it had lessened somewhat.

Hugging herself and using the house as protection against the elements, she edged along the dark terrace. Another door lay but a few feet away.

Thank goodness.

She tried the handle.

"Of course, it is locked," she muttered crossly, pushing a drooping feather away from her face. She'd known it would be.

Ambassadors had many enemies, as did several of the distinguished guests present at tonight's festivities.

If Clodovea didn't get inside soon, she'd become a soggy mess, and explaining her appearance wouldn't be easy. Or else, she'd be apprehended by a guard, which would also require clever justification for her presence outside.

Neither appealed in the least.

Claiming she'd lost her way from the ladies' retiring room inside was one thing.

But outside?

Not believable by any stretch of the imagination, and she hadn't fabricated another story.

She pulled a hairpin from the intricate knot at the

back of her head and went to work on the lock. As a child, she and her brothers had competed against each other to see who could pick a lock the fastest.

She usually won.

Not a talent she generally shared, but in this case, a skill that came in most handy.

It all started when Fernández, her middle brother, argued with Enríquez, the youngest brother, and locked him in a closet. Hearing his cries and him being her favorite brother, Clodovea had borrowed one of Mama's hairpins and freed him.

Papa had thought the contests between his children hilarious, and Clodovea and her brothers had often received lemon drops or some other tasty treat as a reward.

Mama shook her fair head, then curved her lips into an indulgent smile.

Surely Papa could never have imagined his only daughter would ever find herself breaking into a Spanish ambassador's London mansion.

How Clodovea had missed her parents these past ten years.

They had been taken far too soon.

Poor Andrés had just begun his diplomatic career when she'd been thrust upon him as his ward. Fernández and Enríquez were at university, and Clodovea had been sent to a boarding school until she was eighteen.

A few seconds later, the lock gave way with the merest *snick,* and a triumphant grin bent her mouth. *Excelente.* Though it had been years since Clodovea had picked a lock, she still possessed the knack.

Thoroughly chilled, in a trice, she stepped into the room and closed the door. Shivering, her fingers numb, she fumbled with the thick draperies for a few moments before finally freeing herself of their cloying folds.

The smell of a recently extinguished candle met her nostrils.

What?

Her nape hair stood straight up.

She wasn't alone.

All the saints and Jesus too.

She spun around to flee, but the next instant, a large, rough hand clamped over her mouth and stifled her instinctive scream. An iron-like embrace pinned her arms to her sides as the man slammed her back against the granite-hard wall of his chest.

The air left her lungs in a painful whoosh at the impact.

Sweet Jesus.

Help me.

"We meet at last, Astraea," came a guttural, icy whisper against Clodovea's ear. "I've waited a very long time to exact my vengeance."

2

Ambassador Tur de Montis's private study
A few minutes past midnight

Scorching fury tunneled through Lucius Westbrook's blood even as exhilaration quickened his breathing and accelerated his heart.

He had her. By God. He had Astraea.

He'd caught his nemesis at last.

Astraea.

The goddess of justice.

What a bloody joke.

This viper knew nothing of justice or decency or honesty.

Kindness, compassion, and integrity were beyond her too.

More demon than human, the woman struggling in his arms personified all that was evil and vile, corrupt and malevolent in this world.

In hell too.

Astraea wasn't her real name, of course.

No one knew who she really was. At least not anyone operating in the same covert circles Lucius did. She was a master of deception and trickery—a sleuth who appeared as silently and without warning as a shadow and disappeared as swiftly as vapor.

Yet, a few moments ago, she'd noisily stumbled into the ambassador's private study like an inept amateur.

Why?

Her timing was not convenient either. Not with Lucius on an important mission and due to meet his compatriot in less than an hour.

Regardless, he would *not* let her go.

This despicable creature had much to account for, including the deaths of several agents and his beloved, Francesca.

Francesca.

His love. His life.

The vibrant, intelligent woman Lucius had intended to marry.

Remorse and pain tangled into a raw, aching knot in his gut.

He'd even been willing to forego his career as a spy to make Francesca his wife because she loathed the deception and danger. Dear Francesca. Used as bait and tortured by England's enemies to lure him into a trap, then left to die like a rat on a rubbish pile.

Astraea had done that—had left his face disfigured too, though the beard he'd grown for the costume ball concealed most of the jagged line.

Lucius had never told anyone the details that resulted in the scar from ear to lip on his right jaw. He blamed himself for Francesca's death—his marred face a daily reminder that he'd failed to protect her.

Unforgivable and irredeemable.

Astraea even had the gall to leave a gloating note pinned to Francesca's blood-soaked chest, which he'd found when he'd regained consciousness.

In the shadows I thrive, daily gaining more fame;
My foes tremble in fear, for they know not my name.
With a wink and a smile, I completed my mission;
You failed her, Lucius, my unworthy opposition.

Clenching his jaw and with the ruthlessness Lucius was renowned for, he tightened his grip on the wriggling wench. It mattered not that she was a female.

Astraea was a traitor, a villain, a woman without a soul or conscience.

Behind his hand covering her mouth, she gasped in pain.

Good.

It was no more than the Jezebel deserved and certainly far less than she'd doled out.

He had never handled a woman roughly before, but he'd make exceptions to every rule he adhered to as a gentleman when it came to this heartless hellion.

Her grunts and incoherent sounds grew louder.

"Shh. Stop struggling and be quiet," he growled into her ear, pouring all the menace his beleaguered soul held toward this woman into his voice. "Trust me. You do not want to be caught with me here. No one will believe you are an innocent party."

Innocent?

A contemptuous snort burst from him.

There was nothing innocent about her, as they both well knew.

Nonetheless, that certainly shut her up for a few blessed seconds.

Astraea wasn't at all what Lucius had expected, though he supposed each additional successful espionage act further blew her reputation out of proportion. Except for her viciousness. *That* had not been exaggerated.

However, even in the half-light, he noted Astraea wore her signature black.

She couldn't resist, could she?

And why should she?

No one could have suspected the notorious agent would infiltrate the guests. He permitted a sardonic grin to skew his mouth. No one had suspected *him* either.

Why hadn't Lucius spotted her amid the merrymakers?

Likely, she'd only arrived to carry out her mission and wore a costume in case she had to blend in with the *haut ton* guests. Odd that she wasn't wearing her signature mask tonight, however.

Fragrance wafted upward from her hair—a heady combination but more suited for a debutante or a lady of leisure, not a seasoned spy with more blood on her hands and soul than an executioner.

He sniffed the silky strands.

Orange, tuberose, and jasmine if he didn't miss his mark.

He didn't.

His training taught him to note such details. One never knew what insignificant morsel might prove useful.

Fairly tall, perhaps seven or eight inches over five feet, Astraea was well-formed in the places a typical man most appreciated, but not exactly agile and cat-like as she'd been described.

She'd been careless too—extremely and inexcusably for a spy—and that was unlike her.

Sneaking into a room before assuring no one preceded her.

Plain stupid.

A mistake Astraea oughtn't to have made. It suggested a level of desperation Lucius could and would exploit.

Perhaps she was frantic to get her razor-sharp talons

on the documents safely tucked in a hidden pocket in his vest. Papers that proved the Spanish Ambassador played both sides of the political fence.

After investigating to discover what other male guests planned on wearing for costumes, Lucius had attended the ball as a Turkish swashbuckler.

Three other gentlemen wore similar costumes, which played into his plan perfectly. He'd be less likely to be missed; if he were, no one would know exactly who had vanished as the unmasking wouldn't occur until after supper.

He planned on being long gone by then, with this spymistress in tow.

Stabbing pain in his forearm made him suck in a hissing breath a moment before she raised her leg and kicked him in the shin.

There was the hellcat he'd expected.

He gave her a harsh shake.

"Hold still, you witch. I haven't a qualm about knocking you unconscious."

Lucius truly had none.

Hesitation and doubt got a man killed.

Or his affianced murdered.

The darkened room made it impossible to see what Astraea used to stab him. However, the wound was insignificant and in no way deterred Lucius.

They must leave.

Now.

She'd impede his flight, but hell would freeze over thrice and form demonic ice sculptures before he left this prize behind.

"I'm leaving, and you are coming with me, Astraea. Quietly and without a fight, or so help me God, I'll knock you out. I'd relish the opportunity."

Never had he hated anyone as much as he did this woman.

She shook her head and mumbled something behind his hand.

He snatched the feathers from her coiffure and, after throwing them on the floor, ripped the fan off her wrist, tossing it aside too.

"It was most kind of you to drop in and provide me evidence to throw any pursuers off the trail."

There would be pursuers.

He'd found documentation that implicated several high-ranking officials.

The compromised rats would scurry tonight to distance themselves from what was sure to be a momentous scandal and diplomatic free-for-all.

Making furious noises behind his hand, Astraea stomped his foot, only to moan in pain when her slippered toes encountered his boot.

Cocking his head, Lucius squinted at her.

In the muted light, he noted the uniqueness of her regalia. Her unusual costume would draw attention like a beacon on a hill.

"Did you think this mission through at all?" Lucius sneered.

She'd committed unpardonable mistakes.

He would have the why of it eventually, but not now.

Astraea had already made him late, and timing was everything in his profession. By now, he ought to have been over the wall and halfway to the coach awaiting him with his change of clothing. The delay endangered not only his life but also that of Samuel Worsley, the driver.

Sliding his dirk from the scarf tied at his waist, Lucius pressed the blade to her neck.

Whimpering, she trembled against him, and he lashed his eyebrows together over his nose.

What a superb actress.

Lucius almost believed her fright was genuine.

He knew better, however.

Astraea would use any ploy, any means to trick him.

Never again would he underestimate the witch.

"I shan't hesitate to slit your throat, Astraea." Even saying her name made his mouth taste vile. "Make one sound, try to run, alert anyone, and you are dead."

He moved the blade to her back where it was less visible should they come upon a guard.

"Understand?" he snarled into her ear.

She gave a hesitant nod, and another whiff of her intoxicating fragrance floated upward—

scintillating and tantalizing.

Bollocks.

How could Lucius possibly find Astraea's perfume alluring?

What a paradox.

That annoyed the blazes out of him, adding more fuel to the conflagration already blazing within him.

He spun her toward the door she'd just come through and gave a hard shove.

"Go."

Prepared to tackle her if she tried to sprint away, he kept a tight grip on her upper arm.

They crossed the ice-glazed terrace and began the slippery descent to the lower level. Freezing rain pelted them, and the wind lashed and tore at their garments.

The weather certainly had not cooperated with Lucius's escape.

Shoulders hunched against the cold, Astraea shuffled along as cautious and slow as an old woman afraid of falling.

For God's sake.

Lucius couldn't wait to turn her over to his superiors, but that wouldn't happen for a few days. That she'd likely face torture was of no concern to him. He'd seen what she did to *her* prey—*tit for tat*.

Francesca's mutilated face, her sightless eyes

staring skyward, blinded him for a moment, as did the fulminating hatred he held for the woman picking her way down the icy stone steps.

His face also bore Astraea's calling card. The sick, twisted, bi—

"Halt. Who goes there?" a male demanded in a thick Spanish accent.

Bloody, maggoty hell.

3

Spanish ambassador's rear gardens
Five terrifying minutes later

Oh, thank God.

Clodovea was saved.

This man was utterly, completely insane.

He believed she was a covert agent—a…a dangerous and deadly spy.

The situation would be laughable if the circumstances weren't so terrifying and ludicrous. Maybe someday, Clodovea *would* laugh a little about this nightmare.

If she lived to tell the incredulous tale.

But if he thought she was on an assignment, that must mean he was an operative himself.

Her abductor better pray her brothers never got their hands on him. Hot-blooded Spaniards and obsessively protective of Clodovea, they would spare him no mercy.

As she descended the last riser, she braced herself to elbow him in the stomach with all her strength and opened her mouth to scream for help.

"Don't even think it," her abductor grated in her ear, poking her in the back with his blade's sharp tip.

An instant later, he pressed her against the rough stone wall, the hand with the knife encircling her waist and the other at her neck.

Shivering and damp, she clamped her teeth together. He didn't seem the least affected by the inclement weather.

"Pretend we are lovers, Astraea, enjoying a stolen moment. I should dislike silencing him, but I shall if you make the tiniest sound that cannot be construed as passion."

He would too.

Clodovea hadn't a single doubt.

Her breath came in little pants, leaving small vapor clouds in their wake that instantly froze.

Never particularly nimble—no one had ever said

she sailed into a room or swept across a floor—terror made her even clumsier and more maladroit.

The cloud-strewn early morning sky only permitted her the merest glimpse of the blackguard's rugged features. The white turban encircling his head made it impossible to determine his hair color. His eyebrows were dark but not black, and she thought his wintery, cold, emotionless eyes might be blue.

He looked every bit the swashbuckler he pretended to be, from his baggy salver trousers tucked into black leather jackboots to his long belted dark brown leather vest, tied at the waist with a crimson scarf.

Though no weapons were permitted inside the mansion except for those carried by the guards, she suspected the sword at his waist was as real as the wicked-looking knife he brandished and, at present, rested against her spine.

Nothing in the contours of his face suggested he possessed an ounce of compassion or mercy. But then, isn't that what made excellent agents?

Their lack of empathy for fellow human beings?

The ability to carry out atrocious assignments without hesitation?

How did they sleep at night?

Didn't their actions haunt them?

Of more importance at this moment, what did he intend to do with her?

Her mind shied away from the images that so readily sprang forth.

Ghastly, abhorrent, petrifying imaginations.

How Clodovea wished she had summoned the tiniest sprig of courage and stayed with the others—endured the snide comments and scornful glances during supper. At least she'd have been safe from this madman.

What were a few unkind remarks and stinging glances compared to her life?

A second later, the spy's firm mouth took possession of hers.

Shock rooted Clodovea to the spot and sent an electric jolt from her head to her toes.

He tasted of rich coffee and smelled slightly musky but clean. She even detected a hint of Castile soap and sandalwood.

At least he was well-washed.

His beard was surprisingly soft as he moved his mouth over hers in an astonishingly tender kiss.

Given his rough treatment up to now, she'd expected him to plunder her mouth.

Trembling from fear and cold, Clodovea stood rigid as a statue.

Her heart pounded so loudly in her ears that she couldn't determine how close the guard was. Surely the sentinel could see them—could detect her reluctance.

"Put your arms around my neck and close your eyes."

Huskiness deepened her captor's voice.

Clodovea's life depended on her cooperation, and she hated herself for her cowardice and lack of bravery. A warrior would kick and punch, pull this man's hair and beard, scream until she was hoarse, take the risk he'd slide that blade between her ribs and end her life.

Alas, Clodovea was no warrior.

She wasn't valiant or heroic.

No, she wanted to live—preferably without a few additional holes in her person.

"Now," her abductor ordered against her stiff lips.

"And open your mouth."

Open my mouth?

Why?

"He needs to believe we are enraptured," he said as if reading her mind.

Her captor rotated his hips into hers—a silent, angry command to obey.

He wanted to live too, and the unscrupulous rotter meant to exploit her toward that end.

Clodovea raised her arms—my God, they felt weighted by chains—and wrapped them around his sturdy neck.

He was tall and strong, easily supporting her.

How strange was it that at this moment, with the elements bombarding them with miniature icy cannonballs and her fingers and toes numb from the cold, she could feel feminine, not chubby and ungainly?

Perhaps terror had made her dotty. *Loco.*

At the not-so-gentle nudge of his mouth and tongue, Clodovea allowed her lips to part.

Her mind went oddly blank as warm, fuzzy sensations started at her toes, gradually rippling upward over her thighs, hips, waist, torso, and shoulders until they reached her head. A wave of dizziness engulfed her, and she swayed into him.

"You're an excellent actress," he murmured. "Very convincing."

Half of Clodovea's mind assimilated his rasping comment.

If she were an excellent actress, she would've stared down the women who'd sent her fleeing this evening. She would have pretended she didn't care. And she wouldn't be in this untenable predicament.

The other half of her befuddled mind registered that the kiss *wasn't* awful.

She'd only been kissed once before, and that sloppy experience had been lacking in all aspects. This man's kiss almost made her forget she was his captive.

"*Qué está pasando aquí?*" another Spaniard inquired from a few feet away.

What is going on here?

Clodovea stiffened.

Two sentries.

Surely they could overtake the man restraining her.

Well, not precisely restraining her, but threatening her to be sure.

"Shh." Her captor nuzzled her neck, causing her knees—the rotten, disloyal things—to turn to pudding.

"That's it." His beard tickled.

"Nothing to worry about," said the first sentry in English. "Just an amorous couple stealing a few minutes alone, though why they chose out here in this uncharitable weather, I cannot imagine."

"Lust, *amigo*." The second fellow gave a lewd chuckle.

"You there," the first guard called. "Move along. *Rápido*."

Clodovea's captor raised a hand in affirmation, then slung his other arm around her waist as he all but dragged her away toward a clump of bushes.

"Looks like he intends to finish the job out here," one guard said.

"*Sí*, and freeze his jewels off in the process," guffawed the second.

"Not a sound." The spy's punishing grip under Clodovea's ribs brooked no argument, but she must try to escape—not be led like a docile lamb to slaughter.

Perhaps she possessed the merest speck of bravery after all.

"Please let me go," she whispered between chattering teeth. "You've made a mistake. I'm not this Astraea person. I'm not a spy."

"Silence," he snapped, prodding her side with his knife.

Ouch.

The beast.

That poke had drawn blood. She was positive.

Nevertheless, she persisted.

"You have to listen to me. I'm Clodovea de Soverosa. My brother is a Spanish attaché. We only arrived six weeks ago."

"A very convincing tale," the agent mocked. "Your accent is exceptional. Very believable. But that's your specialty, is it not? And I suppose you don't know who I am either?"

She crumpled her forehead.

"No. I do not know. How could I possibly?"

He released a cynical bark of laughter.

"I'll indulge your theatrics and remind you. You murdered my betrothed and left a poem bragging about your conquest."

"That's…" She swallowed bile. *Good God.* No wonder he hated the woman. "That's horrible, but it wasn't me. I swear it on my parents' graves."

Clodovea craned her neck to see where the sentries had gone.

They were nowhere in sight.

Shoulders slumping, she ducked her chin to her chest. Her moment for rescue had passed unless she could stall until they came around again.

They'd reached the outer wall. A locked gate prevented them from going any further. The blackguard probably intended to scale the bricks, but she'd put a cog in his plans.

She'd bet her favorite biscuits—*mantecados,* a type of Spanish shortbread—that this beast hadn't bargained on fleeing with an extra person—a not-so-lithe woman in an oversized gown, to be specific.

"How did you get into the ambassador's office?" the man asked.

"Pardon?"

"Stop stalling. If you're caught with me, your life isn't worth two farthings."

He snapped his fingers.

Neither was his.

"I…umm, I used a hairpin."

She'd stabbed him with it too. It lay on the carpet in the ambassador's office with the feathers and her hand-painted fan. A fan she'd painted herself and that would give away her identity.

This devil had indeed set her up.

Because of his machinations, she looked as guilty as he.

If only she could get to her brothers. They would understand and listen to her. They would help her, no matter the cost.

The spy pointed at the lock. "Pick it."

"I don't know if I can." She'd never picked a lock like this before, and never with half-frozen fingers while wearing a sodden gown.

Didn't *he* know how to pick a lock?

That struck her as odd.

"Pick. It," he ground out between clenched teeth. "We have three or mayhap four minutes, and then we'll likely be shot."

"Then leave me." Desperation made Clodovea's voice reedy. She hated her pleading tone, but pride wouldn't keep her alive. "You can escape. I shan't tell anyone. I swear on my mother's grave."

That was a bald-faced lie, and she couldn't even summon a morsel of guilt at her blatant subterfuge. Madelaine de Soverosa would forgive her daughter for lying.

Clodovea would screech the truth the moment this bounder was over the wall. Except he'd made sure she appeared guilty as sin too. In fact, he made it look like *she* was the thief.

"I *can* escape, but I shan't leave you alive to continue your evil reign." He wobbled the knife at the lock again. "Either unlock it, or I kill you. I assure you that you won't want me to leave you alive for the authorities to *interrogate*."

A nasty smile curved his mouth.

That same mouth that had possessed hers a few minutes ago.

"I imagine it would be quite unpleasant," he mused, almost conversationally.

She swallowed audibly.

He enjoyed tormenting her.

Having never hated anyone until now, Clodovea couldn't imagine what warped a person's soul to such a degree.

Sinking to her knees—her beautiful gown utterly ruined—Clodovea withdrew a hairpin. A thick tendril of hair flopped onto her shoulder.

What did she care?

This man threatened to end her life.

Her lower lip caught between her teeth, and shivering so hard Clodovea could barely hold her hand steady, she slid the hairpin inside the opening. Closing her eyes, she concentrated like she never had before.

She could do this. She must.

Her life depended upon it.

Surely someone would notice her disappearance.

Wouldn't they?

Even now, her brothers and duenna might search for her.

"Ah." Despite the horror of her situation, satisfaction sluiced through her as the mechanism gave way. "It's open."

Her abductor jerked her to her feet and, after edging the gate open a few inches, shoved her through. "Move."

He gave a soft whistle, which sounded like a dove cooing. He repeated it twice more while pushing her before him along the street, taking care to stay in the wall's shadow.

A couple of seconds later, an answering coo echoed through the arctic night.

"You're too blasted slow," he snapped.

She'd like to see him trot down the street in shredded silk slippers, the unfeeling wretch.

He grabbed Clodovea's shoulder and pivoted her around.

"Good night, *sweetheart*."

Derision laced the last word.

"What?"

A mocking smile twisted his mouth as he cupped her neck before giving an intense, hard squeeze.

Then she tumbled into utter blackness.

4

Along a dark, unlit street
A few minutes later

Breathing heavily and swearing an internal dialogue that would've made the devil blush, Lucius lumbered toward the coach at a slow jog. Astraea bounced on his shoulder with each jarring step.

Sam, another covert operative, leaped down from the driver's seat. Hands splayed on his hips, he swung his appalled gaze from Lucius to the insensate woman in his arms, then back to Lucius.

"What in hellfire, Lucius?" He jabbed a finger at her. "Who is *she*?"

"Astraea."

And she was no wispy feather to tote either, even thrown over his shoulder like a bag of grain.

God's teeth.

His lungs burned, and his arms and shoulder ached.

"*No*," Sam breathed in awe, shaking his head. "How the devil?"

"Let's discuss that later, shall we? We were seen. The alarm might've already been raised."

Probably had, in truth.

It mattered naught.

Lucius was a professional.

He hadn't left any trace of his presence.

Astraea's, on the other hand…

Moreover, and of greater significance, he possessed the incriminating documents making this mission successful.

"Aye," Sam said. "Let's be away. We're late."

Yanking his cap lower over his forehead to shield his face, Sam vaulted onto the driver's seat, leaving Lucius to maneuver Astraea into the nondescript coach pulled by an equally unremarkable team.

With a grunt and a muffled curse, Lucius dumped her onto the filthy floor before climbing in, shutting the door, and lowering the blinds.

After changing his clothing, he gagged her with his handkerchief and tied her hands and feet with pieces of what was to have been his neckcloth. Then as an afterthought, he tossed a none-to-clean, ratty lap robe over her prone form. Even unconscious, she shivered, curling into a ball, her knees to her chest and shoulders hunched.

Lucius ought to have let her freeze inside the coach.

He removed Astraea's jewelry too.

Such expensive pieces would be identifiable—at the very least, remembered by the jeweler who sold them. Sam could dispose of the jewels in a way that benefited those less fortunate. He had contacts who were experts at precisely that sort of thing.

Something about the woman slumped across from Lucius tugged at his conscience.

Why, he couldn't explain.

It wasn't rational, and that disturbed him. His entire life, every decision he made, every act he committed, every thought he allowed, revolved around lucidity and logic.

Astraea didn't deserve a speck of compassion or kindness. Not with the list of horrific sins she'd committed.

By God, Lucius would not feel guilty.

He would not.

Not for *her*.

The rest of his costume had already been burned by the contact he'd tossed it to half a mile back. He grazed a hand over his beard.

This was coming off tonight too.

Never leave any clues—unless you want to send someone on a wild goose chase.

Skewing his mouth into a sardonic, close-mouth smile, he shook his head.

He'd finally figured out what Astraea's costume was.

A goose.

And that was plain weird.

What woman chose to dress as a goose?

Mayhap the costume represented a hidden meaning or an inside joke.

The black feathers had come in handy, however.

A slow grin crept over his face when he contemplated the ambassador's reaction upon finding the *clues* Lucius had left him.

She should awaken shortly.

With the blinds drawn, she couldn't see their progress or note the landscape.

They'd traveled far enough in the last several minutes that Lucius was confident she couldn't identify the hideaway's location. Precautions were in place to assure that the inconspicuous lair wasn't near notable or memorable landmarks.

Nevertheless, Sam would take a convoluted route with plenty of turns and circling back to confuse even someone with the most acute sense of direction.

A moan jerked Lucius's attention to Astraea.

Well, where her face ought to be in the permeating gloom.

It was as dark as a moonless midnight inside the conveyance.

She moaned again.

"You might as well sleep. We have quite a distance to travel."

Another two and a half hours, give or take, depending on how much doubling back Sam did.

Astraea made an inarticulate, muffled noise that

sounded very much like a heated expletive. Likely, she cursed him to the lowest level of hell, where she would deservedly spend eternity for her crimes.

With his knife beside his thigh and a loaded pistol across his lap, Lucius folded his arms and extended his legs before crossing his ankles. He leaned his head against the squab and permitted himself to doze.

He'd been up for almost six and thirty hours, and he'd not seek his bed until the documents were safely underway to his superior, along with a message explaining that he'd captured Astraea and asking for directives about what to do with her.

Lucius had dreamed of this moment for years. Now that he'd caught the wench, the fleeting triumph that had sluiced through him at the Spanish ambassador's house had dissipated.

He didn't even want the award for apprehending her.

He'd donate the funds to charity.

God knew there were enough needy wretches in this world.

Now he just felt empty. Drained. Purposeless.

Since Francesca's death, Astraea had been the

driving force behind Lucius's missions. He'd taken the most dangerous assignments, almost as a penance for failing to protect the woman he'd loved. No atonement erased the guilt from his shriveled heart or filled the void that would have been his future.

He must've slept because the lack of movement jerked him awake.

Fool.

Falling asleep with a murderous agent mere feet from him.

Instantly alert, he grasped his knife in one hand and his pistol in the other. Using the knife tip, he edged the blind to the side.

Ah, the hideout nestled in a pine grove.

A simple farmhouse located far enough from other farms not to stir any undue curiosity at the odd hours that coaches and riders came and went. But also close enough to London that missives could travel back and forth in a day.

It must be close to four in the morning.

Tucking his knife into his waistband, Lucius nudged Astraea with his boot.

"Wake up. We've arrived."

5

Inside the coach at the secret hideaway
Near dawn

Furious mumbles met Lucius's prodding.

Had Astraea been awake for a while?

That unnerved him.

Why hadn't she tried to grab his knife or gun?

Perhaps, trussed as a turkey, she couldn't seize a weapon without waking him. Still, that she hadn't tried to harm him or escape wasn't like her.

Lucius descended and exchanged a few words with Sam, every bit as exhausted as he was.

"Get some sleep, Sam. We may have to move Astraea tomorrow."

Sam looked past him to the coach.

"I have a bad feeling about this, Lucius. What was she doing at the Spanish ambassador's? How could she be so lackadaisical as to get caught? The last we heard, she was still in France."

Lucius rubbed his forehead over his left eye.

"That's what they wanted us to think, to put us off the scent."

"It smells fishy." Sam grabbed the harness to lead the team to the barn. "And when something smells fishy, there's always something rotten we haven't discovered."

"You let me worry about it. I take full responsibility." Lucius slapped Sam's shoulder. "Now get some rest. You look done in."

"No more than you." Sam summoned a tired smile before taking the horses to the barn.

Arching his spine, Lucius rotated his neck back and forth, then heaved a hearty sigh. Not looking forward to explaining Astraea's presence to the three men inside the farmhouse, he hauled her from the conveyance.

Pleading widened her eyes, and she shook her head when he bent to sling her over his shoulder. She'd be off and running in a flash if he cut the binding at her ankles and let her walk.

"No. I'm not taking the risk."

His handkerchief muted her infuriated scream as he hoisted Astraea onto his shoulder. Kicking and squirming, she pounded his back with her bound hands while issuing dire threats around the cloth in her mouth.

The door opened, and Ian Hancock stepped out, wearing only his shirt and pantaloons. Yawing, he stretched his arms over his head, the golden glow of a lamp on the table inside illuminating him in the doorway.

He froze, bug-eyed and mouth gaping.

Not something that generally happened to the agent.

Astraea kicked and twisted.

"Stop it." Lucius slapped her on her plump bottom. "Hold still."

Exhausted, he was in no mood for her antics.

She wriggled all the harder, so he spanked her again.

A delighted grin replaced Hancock's astonishment. Never taking his attention off Lucius and his burden, Hancock called over his shoulder.

Astraea writhed and squirmed, and Lucius swatted.

"Uh, Philby. Bernard. You might want to see this." He laughed, the sound echoing across the frosty courtyard. "Nay, you *definitely* want to see this."

Two heartbeats later, two more forms crowded the doorway: Whittaker Philby, a bearded giant of a man who only spoke when he had to, and Nathan Bernard, small, wiry, and fast as lightning.

Three intrigued gazes bored into Lucius.

"Gentlemen, permit me to introduce you to Astraea."

She thumped his back again, receiving another whack on her delectably rounded derriere.

Plowing a hand through his shoulder-length hair, Hancock whistled. "Didn't expect that."

Eyes narrowed, Bernard cocked his head and scrutinized her from head to foot. He wouldn't miss a single thing, and every detail would instantly be committed to memory.

Philby merely grunted, which might've meant, *Well done you.* Or, *I don't give a rat's arse, I'm hungry,* or *I just farted.*

One never could be sure with him.

Lucius strode inside, his irate passenger struggling to escape his hold with every step.

"She'll be using my chamber until we receive instructions about what to do with her." To assure Astraea didn't escape, Lucius would willingly vacate his room and sleep on the floor. "Philby, nail the shutters shut on the window. I'm not taking any chances. I'll sleep outside her door."

Philby gave a terse nod before heading outside.

Lucius eyed the steep, narrow stairs.

There was no way in Hades he was carrying her up those.

He uncremoniously dropped her on the worse-for-wear sofa and cut the cloth binding her ankles before she could sit up. He hauled her to her feet and pointed to the stairs.

"Up."

Astraea shook her head, fury sparking in her hazel eyes, more green than brown in this light.

Definitely not the deep, dark brown of most Spaniards.

More proof she wasn't who she claimed to be.

"Either you walk up of your own volition, or we haul you up wrapped in that carpet." Lucius pointed to the soiled, ragged excuse of a moth-eaten rug.

She blanched and, after sending him a scorching look meant to incinerate him on the spot, stomped across the floor and up the stairs.

Hancock handed him a candleholder, the taper flickering wildly from the breeze caused by the open front door.

"Make sure you secure the house," Lucius said.

"Aye." A single line creasing his forehead, Bernard continued to study Astraea. "I thought she was in France."

"As did we all. Just proves our sources aren't as reliable as we thought."

Following behind her, the generous swell of her hips but a few feet away, Lucius scowled again. He had no business noticing how her hips swayed as she climbed the stairs. This woman epitomized evil.

"It's the first bedchamber on the right," he said.

She stopped outside the door.

It wasn't locked, but it soon would be.

Lucius pressed the handle and toed the rickety, lopsided panel open.

As imperious as a queen, she swept past him.

He placed the candleholder on the nightstand. The farthest corners of the small room remained dark and shadowy.

Astraea stood in the middle of the room, rather forlorn though she held her chin at a stubborn angle.

Without a word, Lucius crossed to her.

Devil take it, he was exhausted and felt far older than his one and thirty years. He still had a letter to write to his supervisor before he sought his bed—the hard, cold floor outside this woman's door.

Astraea winced when he put a hand on her hair.

"I'm not going to hurt you. I'm removing your hairpins so you cannot pick the lock."

Very helpful of her to have revealed that trick.

Once he'd gathered all the pins and tried not to notice the mass of rich brown hair tumbling to her waist, he stuffed them into a pocket. Her hair color alone testified that her claim of being Spanish was false. It wasn't raven black but rather a deep, rich chocolate.

"Your hands. Lift them so I can cut the cloth."

Astraea extended her arms, and Lucius sliced through the restraints.

Outside, hammering indicated Philby had wasted no time in securing the chamber.

At once, she pulled the handkerchief from her mouth and practically raced to the nightstand to pour a glass of two-day-old water, which she drank greedily.

Lucius tried not to notice the narrow column of her throat working as she drank.

"Remove your gown and slippers." Not that the worse-for-wear slippers would get her far.

She froze, her eyes wide and terrified.

Slowly, she lowered the glass. Her gaze skidded to the bed as she swallowed.

Oh, for God's sake.

"I'm not going to violate you." The notion of bedding the notorious spy appealed as much as dropping hot coals in his drawers. "I simply want to ensure you don't attempt to escape."

Lucius would have the rest of her clothes too.

Her mutinous glare would've eviscerated a lesser man.

Bending, she removed her ragged slippers and tossed them at him. They hit him in the chest before plopping onto the floor.

He bent and, after retrieving the footwear, tossed them out the door.

They were useless, the fine silk shredded from their flight.

"The gown." He crossed his arms, enjoying her discomfit.

Her gaze skittered around the bedchamber.

"I…I cannot undo the laces."

Bollocks.

Lucius would have to help her, and he didn't relish touching her again.

Holding her in his arms wasn't as abhorrent as it should have been.

She persisted in speaking with a thick Spanish accent. However, she'd tire of the farce soon enough.

A frown pulling her wing-like sable brows together, she feathered her fingers across her collarbone.

"Where is my jewelry?"

"It will be sold and the funds given to the needy."

"They belonged to my mother." She gulped and dropped her gaze, seemingly genuinely distressed about losing the jewels. "You had no right to take them," she whispered, her voice breaking.

"I had every right. You are a criminal. Now turn around," Lucius snapped, as angry with himself as he was with her.

She complied, but not without another murderous glare.

Rather than take the time to unlace the gown, he cut through the silk ribbons. In short order, the fabric slipped down Astraea's arms, and she clutched the gown to her full chest.

Lucius forbade his attention to drift lower than her nape. "Move."

With something near a growl, she stepped out of the yards of lace and silk. She seized a blanket from the bed and wrapped it around her creamy shoulders as Lucius collected her costume.

"Are you done tormenting me?" Mouth pursed, Astraea looked somewhere past his shoulders.

That struck a raw nerve—a chord of irony. She complained that *he* tormented *her*? The woman infamous for the unholy torture she inflicted on her victims?

Lucius took her small chin between his thumb and forefinger, forcing her to meet his eyes.

"You haven't begun to experience torment, Astraea."

"I already told you. My name is Clodovea de Soverosa, Señor…"

She jerked her face away, lines of fatigue creasing the corners of her eyes and frustration bracketing her full mouth.

"*Dios mío*! I don't even know what your name is."

Anger scorched his blood.

Surely she jested. She must.

Her vile note pinned to Francesca had mocked him.

"Of course you do. Lucius Westbrook. Remember? You murdered my betrothed."

He touched the right side of his face, trailing his finger from his ear to his jaw and over his beard.

"Gave me this scar too."

He splayed a hand on his ribs. "Here too."

"And here." Then his chest.

Finally, his stomach. "And here."

Her bewildered gaze followed his movement, and

every ounce of color drained from her face, leaving her countenance waxen. Her sable lashes fluttered and fanned her cheeks for a heartbeat before they rose again.

Was she going to faint?

Surely not?

It was an act—a performance.

A deuced good one too.

With one hand clutching the blanket to her chest, Astraea blindly reached for the bedpost to steady herself.

If Lucius didn't know what an unfeeling witch she was, he might've believed her pale-faced-and-on-the-verge-of-swooning pretense.

"I didn't." She shook her head, the canopy of nut-colored tresses swaying with her denial. "I couldn't."

"Oh, but we both know *you* did."

He moved to the exit.

"You have two minutes to remove the rest of your garments and throw them out the door. You may keep your chemise. Take a second longer, and I'll remove them for you."

6

The farmhouse bedchamber
Around noon, later that day

Clodovea came awake with a start.

Heart pounding behind her breastbone and angst tightening her throat, she lay still, listening.

Something had awakened her.

Men's low voices.

As her muddled mind cleared of sleep's cobwebs, she stared at the ceiling's rough planks.

Where was she?

Memories flooded her, again enshrouding her with trepidation, fright, and uncertainty.

She lay in a bedchamber in an obscure farmhouse in the English countryside; God only knew where.

Sitting up, she peered around the shadowy chamber. Slivers of light filtered in through the small gaps in the shutters. No sunlight though. It must be cloudy outside.

Not only had her abductor taken most of her

clothing (and her dignity), he hadn't left her a candle either.

"Cannot have you setting the place on fire, now, can we?" He smirked as he stepped from the room, taking the candleholder.

As if she'd be stupid enough to try something so insane.

Clodovea had curled her hand into a fist, wanting to punch the smug smile from his face. A more daring woman might have done, no matter the consequences.

Despite being positive she wouldn't be able to sleep a wink, early this morning, as she lay huddled beneath the quilt on the bed, terrified and convinced she would never see her brothers again, she'd fallen into a fretful slumber filled with tormenting nightmares.

She'd never met anyone as heartless and callous as this Lucius Westbrook.

He honestly believed Clodovea was this Astraea person.

If the spy had done what he claimed she had, even she couldn't blame him for his rage. However, his ire prevented him from examining the evidence rationally and admitting he'd abducted the wrong woman, shredding her reputation in the process.

If she ever managed to escape, compromised and her character in ruins, her brothers might have no choice but to send her to a convent for the remainder of her life to satisfy Uncle Gregoria, lord of Casa de Vargas.

Clodovea pressed a hand to her mouth to halt an involuntary objection.

God, help me.

The notion appalled her.

A powerful lord and not to be crossed, Uncle Gregoria abhorred any hint of scandal, particularly if it tainted the family's name. He might insist on cloistering Clodovea.

Though devout, she had never remotely entertained taking vows. A life of deprivation, seclusion, chastity, and religious discipline did not appeal.

She wanted a husband and children.

No, she would not easily concede to such banishment.

However, there was no sense in fretting over something that might never come to pass.

Sighing, she arose, and after relieving herself in the chamber pot and pushing it under the bed, she rinsed her mouth and wiped her face at the washstand. Head angled, she considered the sturdy, plain white porcelain pitcher.

Was it stout enough to knock one of her captors unconscious?

Mayhap, but then what?

Without shoes, clothes, or any idea where she was, how could she flee and get help?

She could take a man's clothing and a blanket as a cloak, but getting out of the house unseen would take some doing and no small amount of luck.

Nibbling her lower lip, Clodovea tried to devise a clever plan.

An excellent horsewoman, she could saddle a horse herself or even ride bareback if necessary. She wouldn't need shoes for that.

Still considering her options, she padded across the scuffed wood floor to the shutters.

It was too much to hope that Philby hadn't nailed the boards tight as a coffin.

MISSION AT MIDNIGHT

She peered out through the small gap between the slats.

Their backs to her, three men stood in deep conversation near a run-down barn. One agent half-turned and, as if sensing she observed them, raised his gaze to the shuttered window.

Her captor.

He'd shaved his beard.

Regardless, Clodovea recognized Lucius Westbrook.

At this distance, and because of the angle, she couldn't see the scar on his face or the frigid blue of his eyes.

Like fine sugar sifted onto an almond cake, a dusting of snow covered the ground.

She shivered, for the small chamber didn't contain a fireplace, only the chimney from the hearth below centered on one wall. The stones radiated insufficient heat to warm the chamber in the dead of winter.

Clodovea had never experienced biting, bone-permeating cold until she arrived in England.

How she yearned for Spain's sweltering days right now.

She hurried back to the bed and collected a rather ugly woolen blanket. Draping the scratchy length around her shoulders, shawl-like, she sat on the edge of the mattress. She attempted to comb her hair with her fingers, untangling the thick curls as best she could.

Giving up, she plaited the unruly mass into a rope, then tied the end with a piece of lace she tore from the hem of her muslin chemise.

Her stomach growled, reminding her she hadn't eaten anything since yesterday morning, and that had only been a coddled egg, coffee, and a poached pear.

Did the Lucius Westbrook plan on starving her?

It wouldn't surprise her if he did.

He'd threatened to knock her out and kill her, pricked her with his knife, kissed her, did that strange pinching thing that had rendered her unconscious, then confiscated her clothing. Assuredly, starving her wasn't beyond his scope of atrocities.

Clodovea's brothers and Lupita would be frantic, not knowing why she had disappeared. Surely, by now, her fan and the feathers had been discovered, implicating her.

Who did Lucius Westbrook work for —*if* that was his real name?

What exactly had he taken from the ambassador's office?

Something important to be sure, but would anyone believe she was the culprit?

What would the disgrace and scandal mean for her family?

She gasped, clasping a hand to her chest.

Madre de Dios.

Mother of God.

Would Andrés be blamed and his position terminated? Would he and the others face banishment from England? Or would they become suspects and be imprisoned?

Why hadn't she considered the possibility sooner?

God curse the rotter whose blind hatred had brought this conundrum about.

Hot, bitter tears filled her eyes.

If she weren't a coward, none of this would have happened.

A salty droplet trailed down her cheek.

She might never see her brothers again. Nor dear Lupita. Or Spain. Or the Iberian Peninsula.

How long did Lucius Westbrook plan on keeping her a prisoner here?

He'd spoken of turning her over to his superiors. Surely, they'd investigate and learn she was who she claimed.

The key scraping in the lock almost sent Clodovea racing to a corner like a frightened mouse, but something inside her rebelled. Her cowardice was why she was here. What had she to lose by being a little braver?

Shoulder squared, she remained where she was, though she trembled like a newly sprouted blade of grass in a gale. Receiving men into her borrowed bedchamber in her partially clothed state wasn't exactly etiquette at its finest.

The door swung open, and light spilled into the chamber from the corridor.

She blinked against the brightness.

One of the men—the one called Bernard—who'd been below when she arrived last night carried a tray.

Another stood behind him—the huge behemoth with shoulders so broad they filled the doorway.

The aroma of something savory and delicious wafted into the room.

Clodovea's stomach gurgled again, and she lay her palm flat against it.

Marshaling all of her courage, she jutted her chin up a notch.

Enunciating each word with care, she said, "I am Clodovea Madeleine Cayetana de Soverosa, not this Astraea person. I only arrived in England a few weeks ago. My three brothers work for the consulate. Your Señor Westbrook has made a grievous mistake."

The spry man who'd examined her so keenly last night did so again before setting the tray on a small rectangular table.

"Lucius doesn't make mistakes."

What a preposterous thing to say.

Everyone made mistakes.

Particularly people blinded by out-of-control emotions and a lust for revenge.

"Eat." Bernard jerked his narrow chin toward the

food. "We'll return for the tray in fifteen minutes."

Whether it was the suppressed rage, her newfound bravado, or sheer madness, Clodovea couldn't help herself. Forming a wry smile and slanting her eyebrows in what she hoped was haughty disdain, she looked pointedly between the two men.

"*Two* of you? My, you must truly be frightened of me—a mere female. Does that bruise your male egos?"

Two pairs of masculine eyebrows crashed together at her insult.

Careful to keep the blanket around her to preserve her modesty, Clodovea slid onto the chair. She sniffed the contents of the steaming bowl—soup of some sort—maybe chicken. A slice of cheese and a piece of dark bread, along with a cup of tea, completed her meal. Never had such simple fare held such appeal.

Cocking his head, Philby brushed his hand down his beard. "Her accent is excellent—nearly believable as her native language."

Dios, dame paciencia.

God, give me strength.

She dipped the spoon into the soup.

"That's because I *am* Spanish."

Another form appeared behind them.

Lucius Westbrook, his curly light brown hair slightly damp as if he'd just washed.

Dressed casually—his partially unbuttoned white lawn shirt with sleeves rolled to the elbows was tucked into black trousers and Wellingtons encased his feet and calves—he spoke swiftly to his comrades in Italian.

Ah, so he didn't want Clodovea to know his plans.

Too bad she not only spoke Italian but French and German too.

She didn't catch all he said but distinctly heard Astraea's name.

Philby and Bernard left, and Lucius leaned his shoulder against the doorframe, arms folded. Dark hair covered his forearms and peeked from the vee of his shirt. He looked, for all the world, as satisfied as a tomcat with a canary. He slid his keen gaze around the room, pausing for a fleeting moment on her exposed ankle before flickering away.

He was handsome in a rugged, angry sort of way.

Even the scar, clearly visible in the passageways

light, didn't detract from his striking good looks. The sardonic grin arching his mouth didn't either.

Furious with herself for noticing, Clodovea presented her profile and concentrated on eating. She'd need her strength and wits about her if an opportunity arose to escape.

"I've sent one of my men with the news of your capture to our superior."

So Lucius Westbrook was the leader of this small spy troupe.

Clodovea filed that tidbit away. It might come in handy later on.

"It will likely be a week or more before we receive instructions."

Spoon to her mouth, she paused and slid him a glance. "A week?"

Or more?

Clodovea took in the humble chamber. The cracks in the shutters provided meager light, and paltry heat emanated from the chimney. It wasn't a dank, rat-infested dungeon cell, but it was still a prison.

She couldn't even read a book, not that anyone had offered.

He saw her less than excited scrutiny.

"If I were you, Astraea, I'd be grateful for the reprieve. I assure you. Your future accommodations will be much less comfortable. There's a special section reserved for the worst of the worst—spies and traitors like you."

A shiver scuttled up her spine at his brutal reminder.

Nevertheless, as if she wore the latest London fashion and precious jewels hung from her ears and graced her throat, Clodovea elevated her chin, giving him one of the imperious glances down the end of her nose that the English ladies affected to such perfection.

"My name is Clodovea Madeleine Cayetana de Soverosa. My brother Andrés is a Spanish attaché. My other brothers also work for the consulate. Fernández is an international solicitor, and Enríquez is an interpreter. My father was Leoncio de Soverosa, brother to Gregoria, lord of Casa de Vargas."

Clodovea normally didn't mention Uncle Gregoria, disliking name-dropping. But these dire circumstances required using everything in her meager arsenal.

Perhaps if Lucius realized he'd abducted the niece of a Spanish noble, he'd let her go.

Lucius quirked a hawkish eyebrow.

Or not.

"Well-rehearsed, but I would expect no less." He swept her a contemptuous scowl. "Regardless, I'll credit you for a well-thought-out back story."

Setting her spoon aside, her appetite flown in the face of his disdain, Clodovea tilted her head.

"*Dios mío!* Have you considered, for a single moment, what consequences *you'll* pay should I be proven right?"

He straightened and grazed two fingers over the puckered flesh on the right side of his face. "Good try, but your word is not proof of anything."

"*Sí*, but the birthmark on my thigh is. It's unique and supposedly has special significance. Even the priest who baptized me commented on it." Or so Mama had told her.

The priest had also declared that God had a special purpose for Clodovea's life.

The former Clodovea believed.

The latter, she did not.

At any other time, exposing her leg to a man—let alone a stranger holding her prisoner—would've mortified her. But this was no time for modesty. Yanking her chemise over her knee, she angled her left leg. A distinct heart-shaped, rose-toned birthmark lay midway up her thigh.

The heat of his blue gaze behind hooded eyelids scorched her from across the room.

She flung the fabric down.

"I dare you to contact any of my brothers and ask them if their sister has such a mark."

She gave a caustic laugh, gratified to see the smallest flicker of uncertainty in Lucius's gaze before he hid it behind a derisive mask again.

"Of course, explaining how you came by that knowledge might cost you your career—mistaking a consulate's sister for a spy and abducting her. *Tsk. Tsk.* Very sloppy. I should imagine you can expect a severe reprimand."

His thunderous scowl raised her nape hairs, and still, for whatever perverse reason, she persisted.

Clodovea picked up the piece of bread.

"I cannot imagine that will go well for you, *Señor.*"

She took a bite, nearly groaning as flavor burst inside her mouth.

Lucius crossed his arms, causing his shirt's fabric to pull taut over his biceps and pectoral muscles. Not that she made a point of noting his muscular physique, but she wasn't blind. Or dead.

"*You* would have to explain why you picked the lock to the ambassador's office, Astraea. I'm sure there's a perfectly innocent reason."

Mockery radiated off him in irksome waves.

Smug le cucaracha.

Cockroach.

"I'd taken refuge in the parlor next door, but an amorous couple decided to enjoy a clandestine meeting. I'm not a voyeur and escaped out the French window. As you know, it was freezing, and I was eager to find another quiet spot. As I'd never been in that part of the ambassador's house, I had no idea the lock I picked was to his office."

"You can identify these people?" Lucius's derisive

tone indicated he believed Clodovea lied.

Heavens, this man was full to the strong column of his neck in bitterness.

It came to Clodovea in a rush.

The woman in the Cleopatra costume had been Lady Thorburn, the much younger wife of doddering, absent-minded Lord Thorburn.

"It was Lady Thorburn, wearing a Cleopatra costume. She was with a man dressed as a satyr. She called him Tillman or Tipton." Mouth pursed, Clodovea puzzled her forehead. "Or perhaps it was Tifton."

Blue eyes narrowed to contemplative slits, Lucius Westbrook probed her with his intense gaze, as if he tried to see inside her mind. Just as she was about to remark upon his rudeness, he spun around and departed the room with a resounding slam of the door. A moment later, the key turned in the lock, and he bellowed for Bernard.

Clodovea sagged into the chair.

Perhaps a bit of courage flowed in her veins after all.

The same farmhouse
Two days later
Early afternoon

I *must be out of my bloody mind.*

Lucius tromped down the scuffed and dusty corridor, a pair of black trousers, a linen shirt, and stockings slung over his arm. Hancock had finally convinced him to let Astraea out of the bedchamber that had been her prison for the past two days.

Only for an hour—perchance two.

She wasn't permitted outside, but at least she wouldn't be confined in a darkened chamber.

An unexpected and unwelcome stab of guilt pricked him. Where did this peculiar and wholly misplaced sentiment that bordered on sympathy, or perhaps empathy, for Astraea originate?

The hordes of hell would welcome her as a sister in evil.

He was a trained professional.

Emotions played no part in his assignments.

Lucius could recount multiple crimes Astraea had committed, and as sure as there was a God in heaven, she'd engaged in hundreds more he wasn't aware of. Yet, here he was—against his better judgment and as grudgingly as a beggar handing over his last penny—going to offer her a reprieve.

Was he growing soft?

Was it time to consider another career?

He would've left espionage behind already had he married Francesca.

The fierce, gut-wrenching ache that came when he thought about her had dimmed over the years to a dull, melancholic throb of what might have been.

As Astraea's goose gown costume was ruined, she'd have to wear his shirt and trousers. It wasn't as if one of the men could ride into the village and inquire about acquiring a frock without raising suspicion.

Astraea didn't deserve a jot of grace or mercy, but Hancock's argument that she didn't look well grated on Lucius's conscience. Not that he cared one whit what happened to the chit, but he wouldn't have his superiors questioning his treatment of her.

They'd want her hale and hearty for her interrogation.

After Lucius's conversation with Astraea a few days ago, he'd sent Bernard to verify if Lady Thorburn had attended the costume ball. The woman was as fickle as a she-cat in heat and boasted a new lover almost as often as she purchased a new pair of slippers.

Tifton, a well-known rakehell and libertine, *was* at the ball.

Lucius had seen the reprobate and, God curse his luck, Tifton had come as a satyr. Appropriate because the man was an unrepentant lecher.

While in London, Lucius instructed Bernard to obtain appropriate clothing and shoes for Astraea's transfer and snoop around to see what he could unearth about anyone named Soverosa connected to the Spanish embassy. Not that he believed Astraea's tale, but seasoned spies always included just enough truth in their stories to throw their adversary off their trail.

There was the other matter that kept niggling at the back of Lucius's mind as well.

Not once had Astraea slipped out of the character

she'd affected—Clodovea de Soverosa, noblewoman and sister to a Spanish diplomat. She had no reason to continue the charade, yet she did.

Right down to her annoyingly thick and authentic accent.

He unlocked the bedchamber door.

It took a moment for his eyes to adjust to the gloomy interior, made more so by the pouting pewter clouds blanketing the sky and the fusty fog clinging to the ground. Scarcely any light permeated the room, despite the time of day.

Astraea didn't move but lay with her legs pulled to her chest atop the bed, a blanket covering her.

Was she cold?

Lucius might've spared her a moment of compassion if he didn't know the atrocities she'd committed.

In the dim light, she appeared vulnerable. Fragile. Defenseless.

Lucius recognized her mien for what it was—a calculated performance—one that had resulted in many unfortunate victims. One must never let their guard down with a creature as despicable as she.

"Here. I brought you clothes."

She turned her head, her gaze flitting from his face to the garments he held and then back to his face. She swallowed audibly. "Why?"

Why indeed?

"I'm sick of Hancock's cooking."

Slowly, she sat up, the mattress rustling and the bedframe creaking with the movement. She clutched the blanket for modesty as puzzlement creased her forehead.

"You want *me* to cook for you? Your men?"

"Yes."

That was as good an excuse as any.

Lucius would bite off his tongue before admitting to anything else.

She looked away, something like chagrin etching her pale features.

Refined features. Aristocratic features.

Was it his imagination, or were her cheekbones more pronounced?

She'd eaten little of the food delivered to her bedchamber three times a day, though according to his men, she used the clean water provided each morning for her ablutions.

"I don't know how to cook."

What?

Lucius jerked his head up.

"What?"

"I don't know how to cook." Waving her hand in a graceful arc, Astraea lifted a shapely shoulder. "We always had servants to do that sort of thing. I might be able to manage coffee and toast."

Coffee? Toast?

"You probably don't need or want those though."

A hint of defeat threaded her voice.

Lucius was still trying to wrap his mind around her declaration.

She couldn't cook?

Warning bells that had tinkled delicately for days began to clang deafeningly loud in Lucius's ears.

She *couldn't* cook.

Her soft hands with their tidy nails weren't those of a career criminal. Neither was her lush figure, though she might've gained weight to carry out her scheme.

Astraea never did anything in half-measures. She knew her prey, inside and out.

The insidious seed of doubt that had perplexed Lucius from the instant he met her—a kernel he'd ruthlessly and consistently stifled—took root.

This wasn't good.

He'd never questioned his instincts before.

Lucius stubbled a foul curse as he tossed the items onto the bed.

"Put them on. I'll wait for you outside."

He stepped from the room and closed the door.

Resting his shoulders against the wall, he raised his gaze to the ceiling.

A spider scuttled across a web in the corner, and dust moats floated in the air, illuminated by the light coming from a single-paned, grungy window high on the wall at the end of the passageway.

Had his hatred of Astraea clouded his intuition and judgment?

Did he have the wrong woman?

No. Of course not.

Ridiculous.

He'd caught her breaking into the ambassador's office. She had dark hair and unusual eyes—both traits attributed to Astraea. She was the right height too. And she picked locks with a hairpin with great skill and speed.

No highborn Spanish lady—no lady at all—would have that ability.

A portion of his disquiet slipped from his shoulders.

Astraea was slick as an eel, wily as a fox, and untrustworthy as a viper. She was whatever she needed to be in whatever role she played. That's one of the things that made her so lethal.

No, her present behavior, demeanor, and physical appearance were all part of the deliberate deception.

By God, Lucius would not be deceived by her ruses again.

He had once before, and it had cost him dearly, though he'd never met her until three nights ago. Not while he was conscious, that was.

Several minutes passed, and just when Lucius thought Astraea had refused to get dressed, the door creaked open. Her long hair re-braided and hanging to her buttocks, the trouser legs and shirt sleeves of her borrowed garments rolled up, she stepped from the chamber.

Sweet mother of God.

The trousers hugged her supple curves like a second skin, and the shirt pulled taut across her generous breasts.

Lucius couldn't let her go below looking like that.

She looked like a seductress.

His men wouldn't be able to take their eyes off her, and they needed their wits about them.

He grabbed her hand and towed her toward another chamber.

"What are you doing?"

She trotted beside him, but Lucius refused to look at her.

He didn't need that kind of distraction either.

"You cannot go below like that," he snapped.

"You brought me these clothes. I didn't choose them."

"I know."

The previous owners had left a few items behind in

the last bedchamber Philby and Hancock shared. If Lucius recalled, there was a woman's moth-eaten cape—an ugly red and brown plaid thing, which was likely why it had been deemed unworthy of taking. The hideous, outdated mantle would hide Astraea's curvaceous hips and thighs and, hopefully, the swell of her bosom.

He pulled the musty cape from a peg on the wall then thrust it toward her. "Here."

"Must I?"

Oh, yes, you must.

For her sake as well as Lucius's and his men's.

Astraea wrinkled her nose before sneezing. "It smells."

Yes, it did. God awful, in truth.

All the better to ward his men off.

He folded his arms, as much to keep from smoothing a hand over her luscious curves as to present an unyielding mien. "If you want to go below for a couple of hours, you'll wear it. Unless you *want* my men ogling you?"

Lucius gave her bountiful breasts and hips a pointed look.

"No." Face pinched in distaste, Astraea slid the fusty garment over her shoulders.

It wasn't as long as he would've liked, still permitting a tantalizing display of feminine leg, but it concealed her most delectable bits.

Delectable?

Lucius *was* out of his mind.

She fastened the last clasp and then gazed at him expectantly.

"You may only venture into the dining room and salon. I have guards at the doors to ensure you don't try to escape. Should you be foolish enough to make an attempt, you'll be locked—

naked as the day you were born—in your chamber until my commanding officer sends for you."

"*El monstruo,*" she muttered, her mutinous gaze filleting him.

"Indeed. You would do well to remember that I *am* a monster."

She had turned him into one.

He swept his hand toward the open door, and she preceded him from the bedchamber.

"I am curious about one thing," he said.

The matter was trivial and unimportant, but Lucius had to know.

"*Si?*"

Astraea continued walking but glanced behind her, an eyebrow elevated.

"Why did you attend the costume ball as a goose?"

She stopped short, and he plowed into her back, knocking her off balance.

Lucius instinctively brought his arms around her to steady her.

Head tucked to her chest, she trembled in his embrace.

"Let go."

He did so at once.

She lifted her chin, as regal and imperious as a peeress. Hurt and anger flashed in her eyes, the color of the forest at twilight.

"I wasn't a *goose*, you…you ingrate. I was a swan." Her voice quivered, as did her lower lip. "A black swan."

Lucius realized his mistake at once, but the

astonishment buffeting him wasn't because he'd stumbled upon the truth. No, it was her very believable and authentic offense and woundedness.

Presenting her back, Astraea walked on, mumbling insults beneath her breath in an amusing mélange of English and Spanish.

"*El estúpido*. Odious man. *El imbecile*. Blackguard. *El trastornado*. Oaf. *Dios mío!* A goose? Who, for the love of God, attends a ball as a goose?"

Despite himself, Lucius grinned.

He only had one sister, but he was certain that had anyone suggested her carefully selected costume was anything as benign and common as a goose, Althelia would've planted him a well-deserved facer.

That Astraea hadn't only raised more doubts about her identity.

8

The farmhouse kitchen
A week later
Half past four in the afternoon

Standing at a small table and slicing the carrots to be added to a pot of stew simmering in a kettle hung over a soot-stained hearth, Clodovea considered the past week. She'd been permitted out of her bedchamber for several hours each day and had even been allowed to use a knife under Hancock's eagle-eyed scrutiny.

Not out of any great benevolence on Lucius Westbrook's part, to be sure. The fiend continued to make her wear the godawful cape and still looked at her like she had two heads covered in warts and oozing sores. Except, every once in a while—it really was the oddest thing—she'd catch him regarding her with something other than hostility.

Clodovea couldn't define the peculiar expression,

somewhere between bafflement and yearning.

He was the most complex, confusing man she'd ever encountered, and given that she had three older brothers and they had dozens of friends, that was saying something.

She'd volunteered to help with meal preparation and had taken it upon herself to tidy the common rooms. She hadn't much experience with either, but the men seemed to appreciate her efforts, and if it meant more time out of the dingy chamber upstairs, she'd scrub floors and launder their clothes too. Not that she knew how to, but necessity proved a great teacher.

Later this evening, she intended to mend several garments.

That she knew how to do.

Any lady worth her salt could wield a needle with accomplished skill. At least the chores kept her busy and her mind off her circumstances.

In truth, she'd appreciate a candle in her bedchamber and something to read. However, the farmhouse lacked books, so reading wasn't an option. Lucius didn't trust her enough to let her have a candle in her room either.

Each night before she returned to her bedchamber, she suffered the indignity of him searching her person, patting her down to ensure she hadn't hidden a knife or something else that might pass as a weapon or a means to pry open the shutters.

One thing was for certain, Clodovea would never be the same after this experience.

She hadn't tried to escape.

Not only were her captors vigilant, common sense dictated to do so was pure foolhardiness.

Where would she go?

She was a foreigner in a foreign land and would stick out like a fox in the henhouse. She had no money, friends, or anyone to help her. Besides, she suspected she'd not get far before these skilled agents overtook her.

They didn't seem in a hurry to leave the farmhouse, which suggested they had more operations to carry out from this location.

Bernard hadn't returned yet.

The other agents had done so a couple of days ago, and she presumed they all awaited further orders from their superiors.

Clodovea had minimal knowledge of how espionage worked. She fought back waves of nausea and dread whenever she considered what would happen to her when those same superiors had her in custody.

When that day came, she must convince them she was not a spy.

Easier said than done, but with her brothers' testimony, surely a high-ranking official would have to admit a mistake had been made.

If her brothers hadn't been banished from England, that was.

Of course, they would not stop searching for her, but with each passing day, she grew more discouraged. How could they or the people they hired find her if covert operatives had determined she should disappear?

She imagined she wouldn't be the first person to vanish because it was more convenient than explanations.

The first day out of her chamber, in an attempt to gain information by appearing friendly, Clodovea had asked the men all sorts of questions about themselves.

They'd not answered a single one.

It must be some code of conduct or something.

Don't fraternize with the enemy.

It made sense when she thought about it. Anything that they shared, a real spy would use against them. They weren't friendly nor cruel, merely distant, suspicious, and guarded.

She finished the carrots and, after dumping them in the savory stew, stirred the pot's contents. These cooking lessons might come in handy someday.

"Ho, you in the house."

She jerked her attention toward the entrance, visible through the kitchen archway.

"Into the corner with you." Though not unkind, a stern edge tempered Señor Hancock's tone as he pointed to a corner not visible from the entrance. He moved to stand beside her, one hand on the blade tucked into his waistband and the other on her shoulder.

A silent warning to be quiet—*or else*.

As Clodovea very much liked her throat just the way it was, she complied.

Lucius ducked his head inside the kitchen, his navy-blue gaze locking with hers. Every time that occurred, she recalled the scintillating kiss that had unhinged her knees. What kind of woman admitted to enjoying her abductor's kiss?

A *loco* one, that was who.

Satisfied she couldn't cause a disruption, he gave a curt nod.

"Open the door and step outside, Philby. See what he wants," Lucius said, fingering the blade at his waist.

He and Sam Worsley took positions on either side of the door, inside and out of sight.

Whittaker Philby did as instructed and called out a greeting.

"Cold day for a ride, stranger."

"Aye, but I have my flask to keep me warm."

Ian Hancock visibly relaxed.

Did he know the rider after all?

Or…had the rider and Whittaker Philby exchanged secret passwords?

Yes, that was likely the case.

A couple of blinks later, Philby re-entered the house, and the sounds of hoofbeats faded into the distance.

With a flick of his wrist, Hancock indicated Clodovea could return to her cooking.

She'd learned to make bread, and a pleasing yeasty aroma filled the kitchen as the dough rose for tonight's supper. They'd enjoy fresh bread with their beef stew tonight.

Hancock promised to teach her how to make hot cross buns tomorrow.

How an agent of the crown knew so much about cooking baffled her.

And Hancock was an excellent cook, so that flim-flam Lucius mentioned about needing her to cook was utter nonsense. Honestly, she'd expected to remain confined to the fusty bedchamber until she was either rescued or sent wherever the British held spies for interrogation.

"Message from Bernard." Philby handed the wrinkled square to Lucius without preamble before resuming his seat at the lopsided dining table and setting to sharpening the men's various blades again.

"I'm going to check on the horses," the one called Worsley said. Every time his worried gaze found hers, she sensed his bewilderment.

"Hold up for a minute." Lucius waved the message. "This may be important."

As Clodovea kneaded the dough, she kept one eye and one ear on the men in the dining area.

"Still nothing from the higher-ups?" Worsley made that observation, earning him a hard scowl from Lucius.

Lucius formed his mouth into thin ribbons as he turned the message over. "Apparently not. I cannot imagine what the delay is with them or why Bernard hasn't returned."

Clodovea, for one, was quite grateful about the postponement. Not that she'd grown fond of her captors, but at least she knew them.

Well, sort of knew them.

She knew what they permitted her to know, but still, that was far better than being at the mercy of an interrogator.

Particularly as she had no secrets to spill other than that Andrés had a penchant for the ambassador's cigars and usually tucked one in his pocket, and that Lupita was known to sneak to the kitchen during the wee morning hours at house parties and confiscate tasty treats to enjoy at her leisure.

Neither was a particularly noteworthy or criminal offense.

"Bloody buggering hell!"

Clodovea's attention shot to the dining room at Lucius's vehement curse.

One hand on his nape, Lucius stared at the rectangle. Jaw taut, his profile a construct of tension and disbelief, he cursed again beneath his breath, an expletive so foul her cheeks heated.

Bad news, then?

Hancock wandered to the opening and leaned a shoulder against the arch. "Is something afoot, Lucius?"

Philby had stopped scraping the evil-looking knife in one hand across the stone in his other. Though he didn't say a word, he obviously expected enlightenment as well.

Wordlessly, Lucius passed the missive to Sam Worsley.

Features grim, Sam met Lucius's gaze.

"I told you something was off about her." Sam

veered Clodovea a swift, almost accusing glance. "I felt it in my bones from the instant you arrived with her slung over your shoulder."

Like a sack of potatoes.

The men simultaneously turned to peer at her. With one notable exception.

Lucius.

His gaze seared the scuffed floor.

"She's not Astraea," he said, his voice gravelly.

With disappointment? Trepidation? Frustration?

Because he had abducted a Spanish lady after all—not only abducted but held her prisoner?

Surely he'd face consequences from his superiors for his mistake.

Lucius wadded the letter before tossing it into the fire. His expression hard as marble, he put two fingers to his forehead as he watched the flames devour the paper.

At last, his tone controlled and modulated, he answered the questions she silently screamed. "Astraea was confirmed killed in France a fortnight ago."

Clodovea had acquired a reluctant respect for

Lucius's self-control. As accustomed as she was to Spaniards' passionate and emotional outbursts, his reserve appealed in a peculiar way she refused to examine.

"There is no question it was her," he said. "However, our superiors only learned of her death three days ago. A formal correspondence is forthcoming, but Bernard wanted to forewarn us."

Hancock whistled. "That *is* a problem."

Such relief engulfed Clodovea that she nearly collapsed. However, these last few days had taught her that she possessed far more gumption and stalwartness than she'd realized. She would not faint like a wilting flower.

Lucius must release her now.

"Aye," Philby put in, jutting the knife he held in her direction. "*Who* is she then?"

Lucius skimmed his unreadable gaze over Clodovea. "I expect she's exactly who she claims she is. Clodovea de Soverosa."

Gripping the table's edge, she met Lucius's wintery eyes.

"My family?" She could barely get the words past her constricted throat.

Shouldn't she be jubilant?

Gloating?

Shouting, "*I told you so?*"

True, she was free, but her circumstances hadn't much improved and wouldn't until she'd reunited with her brothers and Lupita.

Sighing, Lucius pinched the bridge of his nose. "According to Bernard, your family and duenna were ordered to leave England on suspicion of conspiring and colluding with the enemy. They did so several days ago, under great protest and duress. In fact, they resisted so vehemently that it required an armed escort."

Giving a slow nod, Clodovea wiped the flour from her hands with a small cloth.

How was she to return to the Iberian Peninsula?

Lupita had likely packed Clodovea's possessions and taken them when her family left England.

"So what am I to do?" Arms folded, she didn't bother concealing the accusation in her tone or expression.

This debacle was Lucius Westbrook's fault.

All of it.

He'd incriminated her when he stole the documents and, by default, implicated her brothers too.

"How do I get home? Do you still have my jewelry?"

Though it would gut Clodovea to do it, she could sell the pendant and earrings for passage home. Traveling alone was as appealing as remaining here, but she'd do that too.

Never again would she cower and hide, afraid to face life, because the truth was that had she been braver and less concerned with what others thought of her, she wouldn't be in this mess.

"No." He shook his head, a shock of wavy hair flopping onto his forehead. "I'm afraid not. It's already been sold, and the funds disbursed."

There went that idea.

A tiny wave of self-pity tried to rear its gargoyle-like little head.

Clodovea ruthlessly stomped it down.

Feeling sorry for herself wouldn't rectify anything.

In truth, wallowing in self-pity had brought her to his juncture.

Regardless, that didn't mean she couldn't be infuriated at Lucius.

He had ruined her brothers' diplomatic careers and smeared her reputation beyond redemption. A smudge so monumental could not be wiped away as easily as sopping up spilled tea.

Solemn, their expressions apologetic, the other men quietly slipped from the house.

They needn't have bothered.

Nothing she or Lucius said to each other was private.

"I made this muddle, Clodovea." *Yes, he had, the brute.* "I shall fix it."

How?

Her despair and doubt must've registered on her face.

As he strode toward her, Lucius's long legs swiftly ate up the distance. He took her floury hand in his, an apology in his blue eyes, so much kinder now than they had been even five minutes ago.

Wasn't it amazing how facts could alter a person's perspective?

Turn an angry beast into a solicitous gentleman?

Clodovea was no longer his vile, detested, must-be-destroyed-no-matter-what enemy.

However, Lucius Westbrook was still *her* nemesis.

Had he forgotten that?

He rubbed his thumb over the back of her hand.

"I shall remedy things. I promise, Clodovea. On my word as a gentleman, but you'll have to trust me."

Clodovea threw back her head and laughed, an uncontrollable, hysterical burble that began in her stomach and throttled up her throat.

"Trust you? *Trust you*? Are you rudding *loco*? Insane?"

Tears filling her eyes, she jerked her hand away and wiped it on the fusty cape.

"*You* are the last man I could ever trust. You've ruined my reputation and made me a fugitive, not to mention destroyed my brothers' careers. All because you were bent on revenge and blinded by hatred. No, Lucius Westbrook. I might have to rely upon you, but I shall *never* trust you."

No longer able to hold her tears at bay, Clodovea raced to her cold, dingy little chamber.

Lucius had finally acknowledged she'd spoken the truth and that he'd made a monumental mistake, but this deplorable situation was not over by any stretch.

She was not home and had no means of getting there.

Worse, she had no choice but to accept his help—a man who had threatened to kill her.

Yes, but his kiss had been perversely gentle.

A kiss he took without permission, her offended conscience railed.

Then why had she kissed him back, and why did the memory yet send tingles to her toes?

9

2 March 1826 – three rainy days later
Late afternoon
A miserable, muddy stretch of road a mile from
Hefferwickshire House
The Duke of Latham's country estate

Absently brushing his thumb over his scar as he was wont to do, Lucius regarded Clodovea from beneath half-closed eyes.

She wore her anger and disillusionment like dented and tarnished armor, shielding herself from further harm. Repeatedly throughout the journey, his attention strayed to her until, finally, he'd given up the pretense of indifference and allowed himself to observe her.

Covertly, of course.

A pang of remorse, hot and bitter, stabbed him, leaving an acrid taste in his mouth.

Lucius had never hurt anyone who didn't deserve it

before, and that awareness churned incessantly in his gut. He'd wronged Clodovea, terrified and threatened her, manipulated and coerced her.

Furthermore, he'd forced a kiss upon her trembling lips, and despite the horrendous circumstances, the sweet kiss had rocked him to his core.

At the time, he'd attributed her effect on him to adrenaline, the fear of being apprehended, or worse. Now that he knew she wasn't Astraea, and he'd seen that tantalizing heart-shaped birthmark on her thigh—Well, something undefinable had shifted inside him—had taken on a new perspective and life of its own.

Despite that revelation, Lucius despised himself and held no hope that Clodovea would forgive him. Not only had he falsely accused her, wrenched her from her family, made her a fugitive, but he'd taken her pendent. Something, she obviously treasured and was irreplaceable.

How could he expect such benevolence from her if he couldn't forgive himself?

If only he could visit the past to rectify his imprudent mistakes, neither of them would be here with their futures irreversibly altered. Nor, however, would he have met Clodovea, and though he had many, *many* regrets about the choices he'd made since their chance encounter in the ambassador's office, meeting her wasn't among them.

That knowledge should've alarmed him as no previous menace or peril had—even the moments when he doubted he'd live to draw another breath. That it didn't was cause for reflection—or utter panic.

In his career as a covert agent, Lucius had done many things that would cause an ordinary man to balk. Unsavory and exacting tasks that needed accomplishing for the safety and well-being of the king, country, other agents, and to save his own life.

Without exception, he'd rigidly adhered to designated protocols and procedures until that fateful night almost a fortnight ago when providence had dumped his adversary in his lap.

He should've known capturing Astraea was too convenient. Too easy. Too blasted opportune. His failure to recognize those palpable facts was unpardonable and would require brutal and honest introspection.

Later.

After he'd remedied the colossal conundrum he'd created.

It had taken half a day to make the arrangements to journey to Hefferwickshire House. There'd been clothing to procure for Clodovea, not easily done without raising suspicion, and missives to write, including a request for an extended leave of absence.

Philby had undertaken the task of delivering the letters, one of which had been to Bernard, inquiring if it was too late to save Clodovea's jewelry. Though, in truth, the pieces had likely already been disassembled and sold, just as he'd told her.

Merciless guilt tromped a painful path with spiked heels across Lucius's heart and conscience. If it was the last thing he did, he would replace the heirloom pendant.

Singing carried to him from outside the battered coach.

Sam had volunteered to drive them to Hefferwickshire House. Having another agent along to protect Clodovea was an offer Lucius couldn't refuse.

The vehicle wasn't nearly as comfortable as the

ducal equipages, but Lucius wanted to remain as unobtrusive as possible on the journey. He'd even insisted that Clodovea wear mourning black, including a veil over her face, and had also asked her not to speak except when alone with him.

The risk of someone overhearing her distinctive accent and the ambassador's henchmen stumbling upon that information in their search for her must not happen. Once Ambassador Tur de Montis was removed from his post and exiled—which was certain to happen given the incriminating documents—Lucius would breathe far easier.

Stiff from the last stretch of the journey, he extended his legs and crossed his ankles, his boots nudging the stained opposite bench.

Clodovea didn't so much as flinch.

He admired her poise and self-control.

Throughout this whole ordeal, she'd remained admirably composed and level-headed. Lucius couldn't think of another female—except perhaps Grandmama—who would've faced such hardship and uncertainty with the courage and fortitude Clodovea had displayed.

He possessed an incalculable sense of duty toward her now and must, at all costs, keep her from harm. Toward that end, he had sent word to his superiors that he was escorting Clodovea to a safe location until other arrangements could be made, including contacting her family.

With her distinct features and heavy accent, the best place for Clodovea was Lucius's parents' country estate. She was considered a fugitive until he set things right, which—*confound it*—wasn't easily done.

Not only was Ambassador Domingo Felix Tur de Montis in a monumental rage over the break-in during the costume ball, but he'd also dispersed his agents to locate the intruder, whom he believed was Clodovea. He knew as well as Lucius did that his days in England were numbered if he couldn't recover the documents and prove his innocence.

As there was as much chance of that as the Savior descending from heaven and joining them for afternoon tea and dainties, Lucius needed to conceal Clodovea long enough for Tur de Montis's expulsion.

However, the only way to prove her innocence,

when he'd strategically left her fan and feathers to incriminate her, was for Lucius to admit he'd stolen the documents.

He'd never receive permission to disclose that information.

The directive for his midnight mission to snatch the incriminating papers from Tur de Montis had come directly from the Crown.

The ambassador must never know that detail, however.

Diplomatic relations and all that pretentious rot.

Which meant that although Clodovea's greatest threat remained Ambassador Tur de Montis, he wasn't the only obstacle to overcome. Collateral damage in the espionage business was an acceptable consequence for the greater good, and Clodovea was expendable.

Regardless, Lucius wasn't willing to permit her to be a convenient scapegoat.

So, how to prove Clodovea's innocence and, thereby, her brothers' as well?

First, Lucius must establish that someone else planted her possessions in the study.

Difficult, but not impossible.

A hint in the right ears. A few guineas in the right palms.

She also required an irrefutable alibi that explained why she'd disappeared—which he had contrived but which Clodovea would assuredly despise and probably refuse participation in.

Somehow, he must convince her.

He roved his gaze over her again.

Fatigue shadowed her eyes and bracketed her mouth.

As she had most of the two-and-a-half-day journey, she gazed out the window, her back half-turned toward him. A clear indication she wanted nothing to do with Lucius.

The wretched rain had finally stopped, and the mellow afternoon light filtering through the window bathed her silhouette in an ethereal glow. She was quite lovely even in the ill-fitting clothing—curvaceous, soft, sweet, and gentle, more of a dove than a swan.

Zounds, she'd been offended when Lucius mistook her costume for a goose.

Idiot.

Now that Lucius could see her clearly and not through a distorted haze of bitterness and acrimony, her innocence and refined breeding fairly shouted at him.

Stupid man. How could you, a trained spy who is supposed to be able to read people, mistake her for a renowned killer?

"We are almost to my childhood home."

He broke the stilted silence, his words echoing hollowly in the coach.

Lucius usually anticipated a visit to Hefferwickshire House.

Nervousness accompanied this trip.

He'd sent word to his parents to expect them but hadn't specified the reason, only saying the circumstances were delicate and of utmost secrecy. Lucius had also explained to Clodovea that between them, his parents, the Duke and Duchess of Latham, had eight children.

For certain, Grandmama would find the untenable situation intriguing—a grand adventure to be enjoyed to the fullest. But then Grandmama was somewhat unconventional herself, which everyone attributed to her Roma heritage. Except none of her children had inherited her wild ways.

Clodovea turned her captivating hazel gaze upon Lucius, her eyes rimmed with that fringe of thick lashes that gave her an exotic appearance. Apprehension shadowed those spectacular eyes, though she valiantly attempted to disguise her unease with nonchalance.

"I dislike inconveniencing the duke and duchess."

An involuntary grin kicked his mouth upward at the corners.

"I can guarantee you. It's not an inconvenience. There is nothing my parents or grandmother love more than entertaining."

His sister, Althelia, was in residence, and perhaps a brother or two also visited.

"I hardly qualify as a guest, Lucius."

Clodovea unhesitatingly addressed him by his given name, and Lucius rather liked how it sounded, drawn out and lyrical when she said it.

Uncrossing his ankles, he leaned forward.

"Clodovea, my family is not like many of the *haut*

ton. They are warm, welcoming people, not pretentious snobs. They will treat you like family. Hefferwickshire is the safest place for you at present."

Her misgiving showed in the slight narrowing of her eyes and tightening around her full mouth. She swallowed and nodded. "I have no choice, do I?"

She didn't.

He rubbed his nose and then his chin.

"Clodovea?"

"*Sí?*"

The look she leveled him brimmed with distrust.

"My family doesn't know I'm an agent."

They soon would, but not until after Lucius wrapped up the loose ends and tendered his resignation. Albeit that might not be necessary. After this debacle with Clodovea, he might well get sacked.

Her eyes widened, and her mouth softened into a silent "Oh."

Tilting her head, she ran her keen gaze over his face.

"I shall keep your confidence. I understand the implications to others should you be found out."

That was more than he deserved.

"Thank you."

"Nevertheless, I don't know how you'll explain my presence." She glanced out the window before meeting his gaze again. "I assume you apprised them of the situation."

"I couldn't." Not yet.

"What am I to say to them?"

He ran a finger down his nose. "I've rescued you from dangerous people. No more details. It's the truth, and they are too good-mannered to pry."

Because his family had suspected he was more than an attaché for some time now.

She sighed, averting her attention.

"I loathe deceiving people, Lucius."

"I am sorry, Clodovea."

Lucius shook his head. "I shall do whatever is required to make amends."

Even marrying her.

Daft bugger.

That was Clodovea's indisputable, irrefutable alibi.

The night of the Spanish ambassador's costume

ball, she had eloped with a powerful English duke's son.

Now Lucius must persuade her to agree to the facade, and in precious little time too.

10

Hefferwickshire House foyer
Half an hour later

Standing on the polished black and white Italian marble floor inside the grand house's entrance, Clodovea put an ungloved hand to her stomach. It tumbled over and over and *over*, despite Lucius's assurance that his family would welcome her.

What had he told them about her?

Yes, that he'd rescued her from dangerous people—a contorted, convenient version of the truth—but what else?

Though not a criminal, at this moment, she rather felt like a felon.

Drawing a deep, calming breath into her lungs, she examined the lavish foyer. A floral and gold Spode porcelain urn stood at attention atop the marble-topped rosewood half table in the mansion's entrance. Footmen attired in pristine crimson and gold livery filed past, carrying her and Lucius's meager luggage.

She had no idea where he'd procured the shoes and hideous, ill-fitting chemise and mourning gown she wore beneath a simple ebony woolen cloak or the nightdress and day gown in the satchel a tall footman with a friendly smile presently toted up the stairs.

Nevertheless, she was grateful to have been spared the humiliation of arriving at the ducal residence wearing a man's trousers and shirt, and that god-awful, smelly cape.

Last night at the inn, Clodovea had bathed and washed her hair, then took extra care to pin her tresses into a presentable chignon this morning. Though she might look a fright in the sack of a gown, the Duke and Duchess of Latham would find no fault with her manners.

Beside her, Lucius chatted with the amiable butler whose name Clodovea had already forgotten.

"Lucius." A tall, slender woman with stunning auburn hair and draped in a breathtaking sea-green gown sailed across the tile, her arms stretched wide.

A striking man with graying hair followed in her wake, an indulgent smile arching his mouth. His royal blue coat nearly matched his indigo eyes—*Lucius's eyes*—alive with warmth and welcome.

The Duke and Duchess of Latham.

Even during Clodovea's short stint in London, these powerful peers' names had been on numerous *le beau monde* members' tongues.

Her stomach flipped again.

"Welcome home, darling." The duchess swooped in to hug her son.

Lucius enfolded his mother in his arms and kissed her smooth cheek before embracing his father.

"I was home at Christmastide, Mama. It's only been two months, and with eight offspring, I'd think you'd have plenty of company to entertain you."

"Yes, well, two months is still too long." The smile playing around her grace's mouth belied any real rebuke. "Mothers miss their children."

Lucius glanced at Clodovea and held up four fingers.

"I'm number four. Layton, Fletcher—mother's sons from her first marriage—Adolphus—the ducal heir—me, Leonidas, the twins, Darius and Cassius, and our baby sister, Althelia."

"I'm quite confident that at two and twenty, your sister would not appreciate you calling her a baby, son." Drollness weighted the duke's chuckle as merriment sparkled in his eyes.

Clodovea relaxed a trifle.

Lucius's family *was* friendly and not anything like those cold, unkind women in London.

"Where is Althelia, by the way?" With a hand on one hip, Lucius glanced around.

"She and your cousin Eva are visiting a neighbor but should be home soon." His mother swung her attention to the mullioned window, the tiniest frown creasing the bridge of her nose. "Those clouds look most ominous. I fear it may snow, and I'd like them home before flakes begin falling."

The sprinkling of snow Clodovea had seen in Spain no doubt didn't compare to a snowstorm in England.

"I don't think it will snow other than a light

dusting," his grace reassured his worried wife. "It rarely does so in March."

"Eva stayed?" Lucius asked.

"Yes." The duchess gave a distracted nod. "She and Althelia have grown close as sisters, and Eva wanted to spend a few months in England."

Lucius turned to Clodovea and, by way of explanation, said, "Eva is one of our American cousins that came to visit last Christmastide." He grinned again. "We have a very large family. Father is one of six sons, and I have three and thirty *first* cousins on the Westbrook side."

Homesickness pinched behind Clodovea's breastbone. She missed her brothers and Lupita. They must be beside themselves with worry about her.

God only knew when she'd see them again—*if* she would see them again.

She wrestled the despair clawing at her heart into submission.

Feeling sorry for herself and entertaining hopelessness wouldn't benefit her.

Lucius had assured her that he would contact her

family on her behalf.

Clodovea didn't dare write them directly for fear any correspondence she sent might be traced back to her.

Both his parents looked at Lucius expectantly.

"Forgive my manners. Mother, Father, please allow me to introduce Clodovea de Soverosa. Clodovea, my mother and father, Haygarth and Margaret Westbrook, the Duke and Duchess of Latham."

Nothing in either noble's features indicated they objected to their son addressing her by her given name.

"Your Graces." Clodovea curtsied.

Before she rose, the *thud, thud, thud* of a cane announced the arrival of another.

As she rose, Clodovea glanced across the foyer.

Ah, this must be the grandmother Lucius had spoken of with such warmth and reverence.

Her aged gait uneven, a delightful elderly woman, her spun silver hair adorned with at least a half dozen colorful feathers and combs, made her way toward them.

"Oh, pish posh and twaddle, my dear," she warbled.

Gripping the ivory handle of her cane with one beringed hand, she waved the other back and forth, the many bracelets at her wrist and pendants draped around her neck tinkling like a playful summer breeze teasing a wind chime.

"We don't stand on formality at Hefferwickshire." She winked and curved her rouged mouth into an impish smile more suitable for a precocious child than a dowager duchess. "Unless pompous windbags are visiting. Then we pretend superciliousness and snobbishness to make them feel at home."

Clodovea didn't know if she jested or was serious, so she formed a neutral half-smile.

"Give us a kiss," the dowager demanded of Lucius, which he promptly obliged.

Beaming, the dame glanced between her son, daughter-in-law, and grandson.

"I'm Elizabeth Westbrook, the Dowager Duchess of Latham, but you must call me Libby." She peered at Clodovea through her spectacles as if requesting a commoner to address a noble by their given name was an everyday occurrence.

Which it certainly was not.

"And I shall call you Clodovea unless you prefer something else."

Clodovea sent Lucius a slightly panicked glance. "Oh, no. I could not possibly."

He gave her a boyish grin before chuckling.

Clodovea barely caught herself before her jaw slackened and banged her chest in a most undignified manner.

Who was this carefree, jovial man?

"One seldom wins an argument with Grandmama." Lucius lifted a shoulder. "You might as well concede now."

Wearing the most outlandish fire-flame orange, moss green, and black ruffled frock Clodovea had ever seen, the diminutive woman cocked her head. She studied Clodovea with her birdlike weak tea-brown eyes.

"If you wish it so...Libby," Clodovea conceded.

The dowager made a circle in the air with her cane. "Turn around, my dear."

One did not deny the imposing dame's directive.

Acutely aware her gown wasn't the first stare of fashion, Clodovea did as bid, trying not to wince at the dowager duchess's disapproving *tsks* and *harrumphs*.

Clodovea felt rather like livestock at an auction, and she bit the inside of her cheek to dispel the irrational urge to bare her teeth for inspection.

"I do believe we shall have Mrs. Fillingham call upon us." Libby exchanged a glance with the duchess, who nodded ever so slightly. "The woman and her five daughters are gifted seamstresses," she assured Clodovea.

Surely, the duchess and dowager didn't intend…

No. It was impossible.

"Oh, I could not," Clodovea insisted again.

She couldn't possibly permit them to provide new garments for her. She had no money for payment and would not take charity from strangers.

"You must." Lucius touched her elbow and spoke in a low, soothing tenor for her ears alone. "Consider it partial repayment for your jewels."

He had the decency to look abashed at the mention of her jewelry, as he should.

"You need appropriate clothing, Clodovea."

She bit the inside of her cheek to keep from snapping, "*I have clothing. Lots of lovely, expensive gowns. But thanks to you, everything I own is probably in Granada by now.*"

Except Clodovea had given her word not to reveal Lucius's true profession, and she meant to keep it. She possessed little but her honor now, and a scant amount of that remained after the ordeal of the past almost fortnight.

Curiosity still consumed her about Lucius's reasons for being in the Spanish ambassador's private office. She'd never liked Domingo Felix Tur de Montis, though she'd been mindful to keep her opinion to herself. One could never be too careful when one's brothers worked for the consulate.

Nevertheless, something in Tur de Montis's demeanor bespoke distrust, and when his oily, licentious gaze slithered over her, she'd wanted to flee his presence and have a good scrub in a sudsy bath.

"What do you say, Miss de Soverosa?" The duchess's gentle inquiry made her like the woman all the more for permitting her a voice in the decision. "We could have Mrs. Fillingham call tomorrow. If it doesn't snow, that is."

Flames of embarrassment licked Clodovea's cheeks, but she fashioned a semblance of a smile. "*Gracias*. You are too kind."

"Bah, kindness has little to do with it. Winter has dragged on too long." The dowager gave a sage nod. "We Westbrook women need a distraction until spring makes her much-anticipated arrival. My granddaughters, Althelia and Eva, shall be beside themselves with the prospect of helping you select fabrics, fallalls, and fashions."

"It's settled then," the duchess said with finality.

"A glass of brandy before supper, Lucius?"

The duke's intense gaze revealed the request wasn't a suggestion. He expected his son to explain why a Spanish noblewoman had arrived on his doorstep in little better than sack-like rags.

"I'd welcome a dram." Lucius gave Clodovea another breathtaking smile that accelerated her heart and muddled her mind. "Why don't you rest before supper, Clodovea? It's been a tiring journey."

"Yes. That would be lovely." Clodovea was exhausted, and the merest headache tried to form behind her eyes, even as sadness and homesickness rudely rooted around behind her breastbone.

Maintaining a serene mien had taxed her endurance to the limit.

To her utter surprise, the duchess linked her arm with Clodovea's rather than have a maid escort her upstairs. "Allow me to show you to your room. I think you'll like the ruby bedchamber. The furniture and décor are slightly reminiscent of Spain. I selected that particular bedchamber for you for that very reason, so you'd feel more at home."

A lump formed in Clodovea's throat.

She hadn't expected the duchess's kindness, and it made her realize how very much she still missed her mother.

Libby tottered to intersect them. She wrapped a gnarled, blue-veined hand around Clodovea's.

"My dear, I do not know what circumstances have brought you into our fold. But I *do* know my grandson. You must mean a great deal to Lucius for him to bring you here for a safe haven."

She squeezed Clodovea's hand. "If you need anything, do not hesitate to ask any of us."

Throat tight, Clodovea nodded. Instead of considering her a burden or an imposition, the Westbrooks treated her with unexpected cordiality.

"Thank you. You are too kind." She lifted her gaze to include the duchess.

Her grace hugged Clodovea's arm to her side as she guided her toward the grand stairway.

"Mother Westbrook is right, my dear. We shan't pry, but whatever reasons have compelled Lucius to entrust us with your presence, we are glad to have you at Hefferwickshire House."

Tears burned in Clodovea's eyes.

She glanced over her shoulder to find Lucius, hands splayed on his lean hips, staring at her, his expression contemplative and his eyes glowing with an unexpected warmth that made her nerves tingle.

How had she ever believed him cold and unfeeling?

If they'd met under different circumstances, he might have been someone she could've cared for. Perhaps...even loved.

11

Hefferwickshire House – music room
Six days later – 8 March
Half-past three

Lucius tried not to stare at Clodovea; he truly did. An agent for over ten years, self-control and self-denial had become second nature to him. Like dry leaves during a windstorm, all his training seemed to have flown the way of his common sense when he'd met her that fateful night, and he had yet to regain his full equanimity.

Only she had ever caused him to put aside his strict procedures. He acknowledged the undeniable truth; from the moment he'd seized her in his arms in the ambassador's office, something dormant inside him had unfurled.

When Lucius had believed Clodovea was Astraea,

he convinced himself the peculiar sensation was immense satisfaction in capturing an enemy. Or more specifically, fulfilling his primary goal of snaring his nemesis.

Regardless, once he'd learned of his colossal buffoonery—that Clodovea was not Astraea—the sentiment had taken on a new, not altogether clear definition.

He brushed his gaze over Clodovea, the most unique and fascinating woman he'd ever met. The more he learned about her, the hungrier he became to know more. In point of fact, he couldn't stop thinking about her or that tantalizing heart-shaped birthmark.

Thunderation, he was only human, after all.

After Francesca, Lucius had never expected nor wanted to be enamored ever again. In truth, when he infrequently thought of Francesca these past weeks, the burning hatred toward Astraea and bone-piercing pain had faded into hazy remembrance. She'd always have a place in his heart and memory, but the fascinating woman across the room had unwittingly and unwillingly taken center stage.

Clodovea's transformation since arriving at Hefferwickshire was nothing short of breathtaking. Under his family's cordial care and love, her reservations and prickly façade had crumbled, revealing the generous and warm-hearted woman beneath.

Mrs. Fillingham had delivered the first of several gowns yesterday.

Today, Clodovea wore a turquoise and ebony confection that accented her hazel eyes, made her alabaster skin appear smooth as cream, and her dark hair shine like stars and moonlight had been spun amongst the glossy tresses.

Her recent weight loss only emphasized her lush hourglass figure—a figure Lucius was hard put not to ogle with the ineptitude of a salivating, callow youth.

Even now, his libido surged in appreciation.

More than once, he'd caught his parents eyeing him with conjecture in their astute and mildly amused gazes while knowing smiles tilted their mouths. He hadn't confided his plans to marry Clodovea, but their warm response to her relieved any lingering doubts he might have entertained about whether she'd fit into the family.

No, they weren't his biggest obstacles.

His previous behavior toward her as well as convincing her that a life with him could bring happiness and was the best course for her were the largest impediments looming before him.

Not only was Clodovea de Soverosa an alluring, captivating woman, but she'd also proven herself brave, stalwart, intelligent, forgiving, and kind. She got on with his sister and cousin as if they'd been bosom friends for a decade, and Mama and Grandmother had nothing but praise for the bashful beauty.

Clodovea sat at the pianoforte, Althelia sharing the bench on her left, and Eva standing to her right. Clodovea played with such skill and ease. It testified to her refined upbringing and set her apart as a gifted musician. Last night, she'd shyly admitted that she played guitar and flute in addition to the pianoforte.

She also painted. Very well.

So well, she'd sold her custom-painted fans, slippers, and handkerchiefs in Spain. Pride infiltrated her voice when she spoke of her artwork. It gladdened Lucius's heart to hear it, especially after learning of her poor treatment in London.

Althelia had revealed yesterday that while in London, Clodovea endured humiliation, rejection, and disparagement.

"Some of the ladies in London weren't kind to Clodovea," she said. "They called her fat, and clumsy, and poked fun at her English."

Vicious, jealous hens, always needing someone to pick on.

Althelia had also suffered humiliation at the hands of elite snobs. In fact, she'd fled to America to recover and had only returned to England in December. She would be a true and loyal friend to Clodovea. Spending time with his family helped to heal those hurts and build Clodovea's trust in humanity again.

There'd been no opportunity to speak with her about her fictitious alibi—their fake elopement. Lucius needed to do so soon because a letter from Philby yesterday confirmed that Domingo Felix Tur de Montis hadn't been expelled from England yet. The blackguard now claimed Clodovea had planted the incriminating documents that Lucius had stolen.

It mattered not that his fabricated story had more holes than an unraveling crocheted tablecloth and that anyone gullible or imprudent enough to believe his drivel shouldn't be relied upon to do anything more challenging than pour tea.

It did, however, darken Clodovea's character further, and unless Lucius confessed to the theft, there wasn't a way to disprove the allegation.

The worrisome delay in removing the ambassador from his post must mean the Crown wanted something more—probably Tur de Montis's accomplices.

In truth, when Tur de Montis was finally removed from his post and departed England shrouded in ignominy and undeserved diplomatic immunity, those secretly loyal to him and who escaped apprehension would continue doing the cur's bidding and provide him with information.

More worrisome, however, was that cold-hearted and conscienceless conspirators like the ambassador didn't like loose ends, and Clodovea was a loose end.

It was Lucius's responsibility to ensure her safety for as long as needed—a lifetime if that was what it took, though he doubted this scandal would last long. In diplomatic circles, a new conundrum arose as regularly as a new moon.

With a flurry of complicated notes, the song Clodovea played ended.

Althelia and Eva clapped their hands.

"Wonderful, Clodovea! Simply marvelous."

Althelia hugged her.

"Indeed. I'm almost envious." Eva's broad grin implied no such thing. "Mama despaired of me ever learning to play, and after three years of lessons and much painful-to-the-ears practice, she finally conceded that I have no talent."

She didn't seem the least disturbed or chagrined by the admission.

"I could never master the keys as well as you, Clodovea, no matter how much I practiced." Althelia gave a rueful sigh and lifted a shoulder before chuckling and plunking a discordant chord. "Give me a bow and arrow or a pistol, and I manage quite well, however."

Eva chuckled. "Aye, my cousin and I have that in common."

Althelia winked, leaned in, and, in a sotto voce whisper, said, "Don't tell anyone outside my family about our unladylike pursuits, I beg you."

"Everyone far and wide is aware, Althelia, that you are crack shots. Only Lucius and Layton can best you at pistols." Adolphus's dry rejoinder earned him a proud smile.

Adolphus, Marquess of Edenhaven and ducal heir, had arrived last evening. Lucius didn't appreciate or approve of the keen interest in his older brother's gaze when he regarded Clodovea. That he found her fascinating was obvious and wholly intolerable.

Clodovea was his.

Or soon would be.

She released an unfettered laugh, genuine joy and amusement blossoming across her features and leaving Lucius's heart somewhere in his throat.

"It does my feminine heart good to know a female is proficient at shooting." She speared the other women a glance. "Although I have archery experience, I've never wielded a blade or fired a gun."

"I can teach you to shoot if you'd like."

The words were out of Lucius's mouth before he could stop them.

It wouldn't hurt for her to be able to defend herself if the need arose. He meant to ensure it didn't. Regardless, knowing she could should the need arise might boost her confidence and ease her trepidation.

He'd seen her hidden glances out the windows or behind them when the family went riding. Unsurprisingly, she sat a horse with such expertise that it might stir envy in other women.

Not his family, of course. The Westbrook women wore confidence like a second skin; even Althelia did now.

That hadn't always been the case.

The Westbrooks cheered others' successes and proficiencies, unlike many of the upper ten thousand. Rejoicing in another's achievements cheered and blessed everyone.

"Yes, we could make an outing of it if the weather cooperates," Adolphus put in, giving Lucius a challenging grin as he quirked a superior eyebrow. "Tomorrow?"

The weather had been disgustingly cooperative despite last week's worry about a snow flurry. At present, a few wispy clouds feathered the blue sky, but the lack of wind portended perfect shooting weather.

Clodovea cocked her head and, after sending Lucius a sideways glance, told the future duke, "I would like that, my lord."

"*Uh, uh*. No 'my lord.'" Adolphus shook a finger at her playfully. "It's Adolphus."

"Not Fussy, Fuss?" Althelia teased. Grinning from ear to ear, she explained, "That was Adolphus's nickname when he was a child because he was so particular about everything."

"I'm no longer a child, dear sister." He flashed Clodovea one of his disarming smiles. The one that usually had women falling at his feet and fawning over him.

Lucius curled his fingers against the foreign urge to plant his brother a facer.

His feelings toward Clodovea had assuredly transformed, and a future with her as his wife held much appeal. However, until he received official notice that his superior officer had accepted his resignation or that he was to be reprimanded for his impulsive and imprudent abduction of the wrong woman—hopefully, any day now—he wasn't free to wed her.

Propose? Yes.

Explain the alibi scenario? Absolutely.

Convince Clodovea that accepting his suit was the wisest course of action? Assuredly.

Warn his charming duke-to-be brother off?

Without hesitation.

But actually exchange vows?

No. Not yet.

Lucius could, however, have everything prepared.

He'd already obtained a special license.

There was the matter of what Lucius would now do for his career too. A few possibilities had jangled around his brain for several years, including overseeing one of Father's many estates, investing in the champagne industry, or starting a detective and investigative firm.

The latter held the most appeal, and his cousin, Torrian Westbrook, a private investigator himself, had already extended an open invitation to partner with him.

One ankle hooked on the opposite knee, and an arm slung across the back of the settee, Lucius studied Adolphus from beneath his eyelids. His brother regarded Clodovea with something more than passing interest.

Making an instant decision, Lucius rose.

"I need a private word with Clodovea, please."

Althelia and Eva exchanged a not-so-subtle I-told-you-so glance before nodding. Arms entwined, they angled toward the doorway.

"We shall see you when we dress for supper, Clodovea," Althelia said.

"*Sí.*" Clodovea nodded, the curls hanging on the left side of her coiffeur jiggling with the motion.

After straightening his blue and silver paisley waistcoat, Adolphus rose and consulted his gold watch. "Father wanted a word with me as well. Let's play *piquet* after supper, shall we?"

They could play bloody pall mall at midnight wearing the draperies if only his obnoxious, mulish brother took his long overdue leave.

"Whatever you prefer." Lucius pointed to the door. "Now leave."

Giving him a cocky salute, Adolphus slipped through the opening. He paused on the other side long enough to wink at Clodovea. "Don't let him talk you into anything rash, Miss de Soverosa."

God help Lucius, but at that moment, he did want to pop his brother's cork.

Hands resting in her lap where she still sat at the pianoforte, Clodovea regarded him, her gaze clear and unpretentious.

"What did you wish to speak to me about, Lucius?"

Lucius approached her, unsure how to frame his unconventional proposal.

"Two things. Your family has been contacted and knows you are well, but they have not been told where you are for your safety and theirs. As they are prohibited from coming for you, and communicating with you would put you at risk, they must remain ignorant of your location. For the time being."

She flinched at that revelation but nodded. "I understand."

"I've also learned that the Spanish ambassador has not yet been expelled, and he now claims that you planted the information I took from his office."

Alarm flitted across her delicate features before Clodovea schooled them into a Madonna's mask of serenity that she'd perfected. Only her pulse fluttering like butterfly wings at the juncture of her throat and collarbone revealed her discomfit.

She cleared her throat. "What is to be done?"

Her composure raised his esteem another notch.

What other woman would remain so calm when she learned a madman hunted her?

"You need an indisputable alibi that no one can refute that explains why you disappeared from the ball and, therefore, could not possibly have been present in his office."

"Yes, that would be ideal, but I cannot conceive one that is plausible and will withstand scrutiny."

"I can." Lucius took her long-fingered hand in his. "We eloped."

"*Eloped*? *Us*?"

She burst into laughter, then abruptly stopped, pressing her other hand to her throat.

"*Dios mío*. You're..." Clodovea swallowed. "You're *serious*?" she whispered, incredulous.

She eyed him as if he'd gone mad.

Perhaps he had, and his launch into lunacy had begun the night he'd abducted her.

"Aye." Lucius gave a earnest nod. She must believe him earnest and not merely acting on a whim. "More so than I have ever been about another matter. I've thought this through very thoroughly."

"But surely you know an elopement can easily be disproven." Her wary gaze skated over his face, lowered to his hand cupping hers, and then traveled back to his eyes.

"You did disappear for several days and you traveled in disguise. It might be easier than you think. However, I mean for us to marry by special license in England."

12

Still in the music room
Several incredulous seconds later

*M*arry Lucius Westbrook?
Clodovea only just managed to keep her jaw from unhinging.

Had he been nipping the brandy?

It would be far easier to concentrate and sweep the befuddlement from her mind at his astounding suggestion if he weren't so dashing today. His tailored indigo blue jacket, accented by black velvet cuffs and lapels, made his eyes appear so blue that the heavens dimmed in comparison. It also emphasized the breadth of his shoulders and the trimness of his waist.

She ordered her gaze to remain upon his face and forbid it to edge lower to admire his long, nicely muscled legs encased in black trousers.

Why must he be so attractive?

So pleasing to the feminine eye?

His voice a low, tantalizing timbre that caused delicious little shivers?

It was far easier to dislike Lucius when he wasn't playing the solicitous gentleman.

Nevertheless, Clodovea shook her head.

"I don't wish to marry you or live in England. I also do not believe, for all the lace in Spain, that you have any desire to tie yourself to me for a lifetime either, Lucius."

"It is the soundest and most credible option, Clodovea."

Sound. Credible.

My, wasn't that as romantic and tempting as stepping in fresh cow manure?

Lucius brushed his callused thumb over the back of her hand.

She really should pull her hand away, but she liked how his big palm engulfed hers—enjoyed the warmth and tingles that flitted up her arm at his touch.

"I must disagree, Lucius. It would be the height of folly."

Only a foolish nitwit would allow his charm to sway her.

Marriage to a stranger?

Well, not quite a stranger now, but still by no means an ideal candidate for a marriage of convenience. Besides, Clodovea well knew that only guilt motivated him to make the ridiculous declaration. Undoubtedly, he believed sacrificing himself on the altar of matrimony, a noble gesture, would atone for his previous hostile and abhorrent behavior.

She supposed that his proposition was chivalrous to a degree. But she neither needed nor wanted gallantry. What she yearned for was for her reputation to be restored and to be reunited with her family. There was scant chance of the former, and the latter proved highly challenging at present too.

A half-smile lighting his eyes, Lucius continued as if he hadn't heard her objection.

"It's the most reasonable solution and will keep you safest, Clodovea."

He leaned in and lowered his voice. "I've resigned from my position too. I cannot continue as an agent once

I'm married. I haven't heard from my superiors yet, but once I do, we should wed without delay."

Lucius swerved a swift, leery glance to the partially open door.

Did he worry that someone listened outside?

Did they?

As loving and accepting as his family appeared, Clodovea didn't think they would object to his occupation. But then again, mayhap, worry about their safety prompted his caution.

Espionage was a notoriously nasty business.

In all probability, Lucius had scores of enemies other than Astraea.

Tugging at his earlobe, he gave her a sideways look. Both hopeful and uncertain.

"Well? What say you?"

Lucius's sincerity came as a surprise.

He offered Clodovea security and a way to remove a bit of the tarnish from her name. She brought him nothing, for she suspected Uncle Gregoria would consider her dowry forfeit for smudging the de Soverosa name. Her brothers mightn't be keen on her wedding an

Englishman either, though the subject had never arisen in conversation.

She put a finger to her mouth and pressed her lips together in consternation.

"I honestly don't know, Lucius."

Lord, Clodovea truly didn't.

Marrying Lucius would be rash. Imprudent. Reckless.

She was none of those things.

Self-preservation screeched loudly in her ears to bolt from the room.

Instead, Clodovea closed her eyes and put two fingers to the bridge of her nose as she sometimes did when in deep contemplation. "I have never wanted or considered for two minutes that I'd ever enter a marriage of convenience."

She'd always hoped for a love match like Mama and Papa.

A marriage of convenience was a small step above an arranged marriage, which she'd always regarded as calculated and cold.

Either might work well for other people but not for

Clodovea. She was too much of a romantic. It didn't help that her parents had been devoted to each other, and she knew from observing them how wonderful a loving union could be.

A flash of bare limbs and echoes of passionate moans intruded upon her musings.

Just look at Lady Thorburn.

Lady, indeed.

Unfaithful, fickle, and making a cuckold of Lord Thorburn. And her ladyship wasn't alone in her adultery. Unfaithfulness was acceptable among Society's upper crust, as long as one was discreet, of course.

Clodovea nibbled her lower lip.

Nevertheless, marriage to Lucius was preferable to being locked behind a nunnery's imposing walls for a lifetime.

Would Uncle Gregoria force that fate upon her?

Her brothers?

It wasn't impossible. Uncle was somewhat of a zealot.

She'd run away first.

Where to?

If you married Lucius, you wouldn't have to run away, Clodovea Madeleine Cayetana de Soverosa.

Clodovea must be out of her mind for even considering Lucius's proposal for half a second.

This man had abducted her—had threatened to kill her. Had bound and gagged her.

Yes, but he'd believed she was his archenemy at that time. A murderous spy. Once he'd discovered his error, Lucius had treated her with nothing but kindness and consideration.

She fingered the silk ribbon on her sleeve, her eyes firmly shut. It was easier to think when Lucius's beautiful eyes weren't caressing her, causing her thoughts to scramble over themselves.

"No one will believe it," she murmured, thinking aloud.

How could they?

She couldn't believe Lucius thought their marrying was the best solution. "Not your family. Not mine. Not the authorities."

"We'll claim we've been secretly seeing each

other, and we fled to Scotland and wed over an anvil," he said.

Oh, there was *nothing* suspicious about that at all. If Clodovea's eyes hadn't been closed, she would've rolled them in exaggerated sarcasm.

"Because you wanted a cleric to perform the ceremony to alleviate any doubt as to the authenticity of the union, we exchanged vows again in England. My family can act as witnesses. We will be legally married."

Opening her eyes, Clodovea angled her head, tracing her gaze over the scar slashing Lucius's face before meeting those alarmingly blue eyes.

The gash must've hurt something awful.

"How did Astraea do that to you?"

She pointed at his scar with her gaze.

Lucius remained silent for several *tick-tocks* of the fern-green Wedgewood ormolu mantel clock. She sighed and gently placed her hand upon her thigh before leaning an elbow on the pianoforte and staring out into the bleak and barren rose garden visible beyond the tall windows.

"She lured my intended into a trap with the

intention of snaring me. Astraea tortured and killed Francesca, left me with this scar, and the others I told you about."

He flicked a long finger, indicating the ragged flesh. A sardonic smile hitched his mouth upward at the corners.

"Astraea found perverse joy in carving up her victims. I should've died, but by some miracle did not."

Shock sent a shudder reverberating through Clodovea, and she gasped.

"*Dios mío*! No wonder you despised her."

How could anyone be that vile?

Clodovea had never loathed someone she'd never met before, but she despised this Astraea person—was glad the spy was dead and couldn't ever harm Lucius or his loved ones again.

A muscle worked in his jaw as he relived the traumatic event.

Wanting to soothe him, Clodovea laid her hand atop his on the pianoforte's shiny wooden surface.

"I can only promise to consider your offer, Lucius. I think too much has passed between us to have a successful marriage." She notched her chin higher. "I shall not exchange one undesirable situation for another. Most especially not one that lasts a lifetime and from which I could never escape."

Like being imprisoned in a convent.

"I understand." He gave a taut dip of his strong chin and stepped aside as she rose from the bench. "I shall respect your decision for now, but I shan't give up."

Clodovea nodded as she passed Lucius, involuntarily inhaling his cologne and a hint of shaving lather too. She needed time alone. Time to process his impossible request and digest the fact that through no fault of theirs, her family would not be coming to rescue her.

"Clodovea?"

"*Si?*" She half-turned, willing her emotions not to betray her.

"Can you ever forgive me?" Sincerity and a touch of angst made Lucius's voice husky. "For everything? Even the loss of your pendant? I know I don't deserve it, but I covet your forgiveness."

Forgive him?

For *everything*?

Again, she searched his face.

A noble face. A rugged face. A face etched with authentic regret and blue, blue eyes that held a wisp of hope.

Can I?

"Perhaps." She must. For her sake as well as his. If she harbored anger and resentment, they'd grow into bitterness. She'd be no better than the mean-spirited ladies who'd teased and taunted her.

Yes, the loss of her mother's pendant grieved her, but it was after all, just a piece of jewelry. Surely, if she could forgive Lucius for his other offences against her, she could forgive him that too.

With God, all things are possible.

Yes, but that didn't mean they were easy or even desirable.

In truth, Clodovea was more than halfway to forgiving Lucius, especially after learning why he'd acted as he had. But something, mayhap self-preservation, kept her from admitting that detail to him.

She had scant control over any aspect of her life,

and this man who had upended it couldn't be allowed to manipulate her emotions. Something, she feared, he could do with a flick of his wrist unless she fortified her parapets against his debonair charm.

Because *this* Lucius was deucedly tempting.

"I'll seriously consider that as well," she said softly.

Complete, unconditional forgiveness would set both of them free.

"Consider what?"

Libby tottered into the room wearing a shocking red, yellow, blue, and pink gown that quite took one's breath away at first glance. In her bright plumage, she rather resembled a tropical bird.

Carrying a small ornate box tied with a bright scarlet ribbon in one hand, she clutched her ever-present cane in the other. As was her wont, she wore a swath of jewelry that chinked and tinkled with her labored steps.

Clodovea sent a panicked, pleading glance to Lucius.

Completely unperturbed, he gave his grandmother a boyish grin.

"I'm teaching Clodovea how to shoot tomorrow

and suggested she might enjoy learning how to wield a blade as well."

How easily lies fell from Lucius's lips. But then again, what agent worth his salt told the truth?

Spying entailed subterfuge, ruses, and cons.

Could she marry such a man?

Libby beamed in approval.

"Good for you, Clodovea. I used to have considerable skill with a knife. Many Roma do." She thrust the box outward. "Turkish delight? Doctor Hartney, the elder, spoils me with the occasional box even while his son lectures me to avoid sweets."

"*Sí*. I shall try a piece." Clodovea had heard about the scrumptious treat but had never tasted it. She selected a small square and dropped it into her mouth.

Scrumptious.

She closed her eyes briefly before popping her lids back open and grinning.

"Mmm. *Marvilloso*. That may be the most delicious thing I have ever tasted."

"Not for me." Lucius shook his head. "I have correspondence I must see to."

The long, speaking glance he gave Clodovea said he wasn't done discussing marriage.

She wasn't sure whether to be alarmed or enthralled.

He gave a short bow. "Please excuse me."

His grandmother watched him leave the room before turning her astute gaze on Clodovea.

"My dear, I must confess. I eavesdropped upon your conversation with Lucius."

Oh, bother.

This was awkward.

An eyebrow quirked, Clodovea eyed her.

Just *how* much had the grand dame overheard?

Eyes twinkling and not the least abashed by her admission, the dowager curved her mouth.

"At four and eighty, I have tossed aside most starchy conventions and do as I deuced well please." Chuckling, a rasp like the crinkling of old paper, she winked. "Truthfully, I've cocked a snook at Society most of my life."

Clodovea wasn't surprised. The woman was the most delightfully precocious and charmingly unconventional creature she'd ever met.

Peering up at her, the dowager asked, "What does my grandson need forgiveness for?"

Indecision warred within Clodovea for several heartbeats. She couldn't tell the dowager everything, but it would be wonderful to talk to someone.

"You had best sit down, Libby."

It still seemed wrong to address the dowager duchess by her pet name.

"Oh, this is going to be tremendous. I just know it." Like a child who'd discovered a secret, the elderly woman beamed as she tottered to the settee.

Once settled side by side, Clodovea outlined the basics, keeping the more intimate details like the kiss and exposing her birthmark to herself. She also did not reveal that Lucius was a spy. Instead, she improvised and said he wrongly believed he'd caught a thief and a spy and, rather than turn her over to the authorities, believed it wiser to inform his superiors. He was a soldier, after all.

At least, that was the persona he presented to the world.

"Once Lucius realized his mistake and that I was exactly who I said I was, he determined to set things to right straightaway."

The dowager made a sympathetic sound and patted Clodovea's knee.

"There you have it, Libby."

She clasped her cold hands together, relieved to have told a portion of the truth.

"I cannot go home because I'm a fugitive." She lifted a shoulder and curved her mouth into a half-sad, half-wry smile.

"And my family cannot come for me. Lucius thinks he's being honorable and making amends by offering me marriage as well as protecting me. But I don't want that sort of shadow hanging over me. Over us."

If—and that was a very small, dubious if—they married.

Expression kind and reflective, Libby grasped her cane's ivory handle with both hands.

"My marriage was an arranged marriage, and Margaret and Haygarth's was a marriage of convenience." She gave a sage nod, wisdom and melancholy glowing in her eyes. "I came to adore my husband and loved Gerhardt until the Good Lord took him home. Of course, you've seen how Margaret and Garth look at each other."

Clodovea nodded.

Yes, she had. It reminded her of her parents' loving union.

And yet, doubt persisted. "But there is no guarantee, is there?"

Libby snorted and flapped her arthritic hand back and forth.

"There is no guarantee of *anything* in life. But this I know." She thumped her cane, and Clodovea jumped.

"If both spouses are willing to give the union a chance and are committed to making it successful while respecting and honoring the other, love has a sneaky way of creeping in when you least expect it and stealing hearts." A dreamy look entered the dowager duchess's weak eyes. "Your spirits become one."

That might be so, but many arranged marriages and marriages of convenience proved disastrous, with the couples despising one another or becoming completely apathetic toward the other.

Which was worse?

Clodovea's musings must've shown on her face because the dowager patted Clodovea's knee with her crepey, gnarled hand.

"Lucius never does anything by half measure and never without considering the entire spectrum of consequences. If he proposed, it's because he *wants* to marry you, my dear. Even if *he* doesn't realize it yet."

She gave another convincing bob of her silvery head.

"Perhaps," Clodovea murmured, still unconvinced.

But perhaps not.

She had much to contemplate. "If you'll excuse me, please. I would benefit from some time alone. It's all been a bit overwhelming."

A bit?

No, she'd been utterly confounded.

"Oh, and please don't discuss anything I shared with you." She covered Libby's hand with hers. "I'm not quite ready for the rest of the family to know the…ah, *unique* circumstances behind Lucius and me meeting."

"Of course not, my dear." Libby kissed Clodovea's cheek. "I hope you'll say yes. I'd very much like to have you as a granddaughter. I think we are much alike."

Libby would've set society on its ear when she was younger.

Clodovea grinned. "I am honored that you think so."

13

Hefferwickshire House
The next afternoon
Shooting lessons on the south lawn

Lucius tossed Adolphus an unrepentant, triumphant grin as his brother grumbled something ungentlemanly beneath his breath and accepted a loaded pistol from an expressionless footman.

Clodovea had agreed to permit Lucius to help her learn to shoot and not his eager sibling.

The attention Adolphus slathered on Clodovea grated on Lucius's nerves, and unfamiliar jealousy sunk her sharp talons into his heart.

Farther along the greens, Althelia and Eva trained their pistols at targets fifty feet away. Practiced shooters, each hit their mark dead center nearly every time they fired, as did Adolphus.

Clodovea, however, flinched when she pulled the

trigger, causing the lead ball to go wide.

Lucius stepped behind her and spoke into her ear. "Don't hold your breath or tense your body."

"Uh, hum." Forehead furrowed, she squinted at the target. "It's so loud, and the pistol feels heavy and awkward."

The sound was deafening to someone unaccustomed to a gun's blast, and it did take time to learn to balance the weapon in one's hand.

"Here. Put these in your ears." Lucius handed her two small pieces of cloth. "They should help until you become accustomed to the sound."

Glancing up at him over her shoulder, she gave him a grateful smile as she tucked the scraps into her shell-like ears. She wore no earrings, and guilt needled him once more.

He had Bernard trying to recover her jewelry, but there was little chance the pendant and earrings hadn't been disassembled and the bits and bobs sold. That was the nature of fencing jewels.

Lucius's gaze locked with Clodovea's, and a scintillating current—smoldering, profound, undeniable—passed between them.

Her pupils dilated, and her full lips parted in awareness.

Very interesting. And very heartening.

From the beginning, he'd suspected Clodovea wasn't any more immune to him than Lucius was to her. Now that they weren't avowed enemies, he had every intention of stoking that provocative interest.

Desire was an excellent foundation for marriage—not the only basis, of course.

"Are you two going to stand there all day, or are you going to shoot?" Adolphus's disgruntled question broke the interlude.

Lucius cocked an eyebrow in askance. "Give us a moment, big brother."

Moodiness and surliness weren't typical behaviors for Adolphus. As the ducal heir, he'd lived a privileged life and had seldom been denied anything. Not that their parents had treated him any differently than their seven other children.

No. *Le Beau Monde* was responsible for placing Adolphus upon a lofty perch. He didn't always appreciate the fawning, but it hadn't prepared him to be thwarted in romance very often.

Looking like a piece of plump, delectable fruit in a tangerine-colored redingote, Clodovea caught her lower lip between her small white teeth and crinkled her nose in the adorable fashion she did when concentrating.

Copying Althelia and Eva, she'd removed her bonnet and placed it on a nearby bush lest the slight breeze catch the ribbons and distract or interfere with her aim.

Lucius rested one hand on her shoulder and cupped the elbow of her extended arm with his other.

She trembled.

From the contact or anticipation of the gun's loud report?

"Steady," he breathed into her ear. "You can do this."

She smelled of perfumed soap—probably a gift from Mama or Althelia.

Lucius preferred the scent she'd worn that first night: **oranges, tuberose, and jasmine.**

Sweet, alluring, and seductive, yet innocent.

The epitome of Clodovea.

"Look down the muzzle to the point where you want the ball to hit. Inhale, and when you've released the breath, pull the trigger."

She gave a little nod, brushing her satiny hair against his face.

Equal parts torture and bliss.

Her shoulders rose as she breathed in, then sank as she exhaled. She pulled the trigger and an instant later, the ball slammed into the target, only eight inches from the center.

"Well done, you," Althelia called as she accepted another loaded pistol.

Eva released a boisterous and most unladylike whistle. "Brilliant, Clodovea."

Raised in America, she tended to be a jot more exuberant than English society approved of.

Althelia had picked up a few of her American cousin's habits, which had done her well. No longer did she fear what others thought of her.

Adolphus gave an approving nod. "I knew you'd catch on."

The footmen smiled in approval too.

Guileless and unpretentious, Clodovea had a way of wriggling into everyone's heart and good graces.

"I did it!" Clodovea gave a little hop and pivoted to face Lucius, her eyes shining.

"I did it, Lucius."

Excitement emphasized her accent, drawing out each lilting syllable.

Her radiant smile nearly blinded him, and with his attention fixated on her pretty eyes, his heart toppled from his chest and lay, exposed and vulnerable at her feet.

My God.

Lucius had done the bloody untenable.

The deuced unthinkable.

He'd fallen in love with Clodovea.

Remarkable, unique, unpredictable, gentle, unaffected Clodovea.

That was what this weird sensation was tunneling through his veins, invading his mind, and squeezing his heart. *Love.* Unforeseen, unmerited, but wholly welcome and cherished.

Glee danced a spirited jig behind his ribs even as Lucius's mind fervently whispered, *Take heed. Proceed with caution. Rely upon your training. The heart is not logical and cannot be relied upon.*

All true, but at the moment, Lucius didn't give a devil's damn.

He was in love.

Something he'd never expected to feel again, and he simultaneously wanted to shout the epiphany to the skies and yet tuck it away in his heart to savor.

He couldn't have constrained his smile or prevented himself from flicking the coffee-colored curl teasing her ear if his life depended on it.

"You certainly did, little dove."

Her eyes softened at the term of endearment.

Just as Clodovea opened her mouth to respond, a blast of wind whipped the women's skirts about their ankles and sent the footmen's tailcoats fluttering like cardinals' wings.

Training a practiced gaze upon the sky, Lucius narrowed his eyes.

A flurry of clouds from the west portended a spring storm.

"We'd best make our way inside," Adolphus said, striding toward the table where the gun cases lay open. He directed his gaze to the fast-moving pewter clouds bearing down upon them. "That squall will be upon us shortly."

Spreading her arms wide, Eva raised her face. "I adore a good storm as long as I am inside. The northeasters we have in America are quite something."

"They are, indeed." Althelia agreed as she collected her bonnet, then handed Eva hers. "I prefer England's showers to those battering tempests." She gave a delicate shudder. "I've never heard the wind howl so. It made the hair on my arms stand on end."

With swift efficiency, the guns were returned to their respective cases, and Adolphus toted them inside as the footmen carried the table behind him.

The wind snatched Clodovea's bonnet off the bush.

"Oh, dear. My bonnet."

"I'll retrieve it." Lucius sprinted after the hat, tumbling pell-mell over the green. Several feet away, he managed to grasp a fluttering orange ribbon.

Great drops of rain splattered from the sky, slowly

at first but with increasing speed as the seconds ticked on.

They were in for a good soaking if they didn't hurry inside.

"Go on with you." Clodovea waved at Althelia and Eva, who waited patiently for her. "I should hate for the rain to ruin your garments or for you to become chilled."

She glanced toward Lucius as he approached, bonnet in hand. "We'll be along shortly."

"We'll have tea prepared," Althelia said with a nod. "We can play cards or charades to pass the rest of the afternoon."

Their bonnets hanging from their forearms by their ribbons, Althelia and Eva linked their other arms and hurried to the house. The wind snatched at their redingotes and gowns with the ferocity of a starving dog seizing a piece of bread.

"I'd rather be tarred and feathered than play charades," Lucius muttered as he approached Clodovea.

"I rather like them," Clodovea said softly.

He grinned and offered her his arm. "Then charades it is."

Lucius rather feared if she asked for the stars in the sky, he'd find a way to net them and present them to her on a salver.

She reached for her bonnet before placing her hand on his forearm.

"I'll carry it for you."

A particularly large raindrop landed on her nose, and she laughed, her eyes bright as she swiped it away.

Lucius drew her into his embrace. "I love hearing you laugh."

She stilled, her warm hazel gaze searching his.

Slowly, giving her time to pull away, he lowered his mouth to hers.

This melding of their mouths would be much different than the punishing kiss that first night. When he'd wanted to exact revenge. He poured all of his reverence and adoration into the caress.

He barely brushed his lips across the velvety mounds.

Once. Twice. Thrice.

Clodovea's breath quickened, but she didn't pull away. Instead, she angled her chin to allow him better access to her mouth's sweetness. Her eyelashes fluttered before fanning across her cheeks, and she dug her fingers into his arms.

Though greedy for more—ravenous, in truth, to worship her body with his—Lucius was determined to take things slowly. To woo Clodovea properly. He had much harm to undo.

After sweeping her mouth with his once more, he whispered in her ear, "We better go inside. The others will wonder where we are."

Her lashes trembled, and then she raised her eyelids.

Eyes round with wonder and a touch of pleased confusion, she placed two fingers on her lips.

"Why did you kiss me?"

"Because, my little dove, you tempt me beyond self-control." He winked. "And I promise you, I am unfamiliar with that."

Lord, was that ever the truth.

Speculation causing a crease above her nose, Clodovea eyed him, assuredly attempting to read his mind—his motives.

Lucius could almost see and hear the wheels and cogs turning and grinding inside her brain as she endeavored to discern if he spoke the truth.

Finally, a nascent smile that told him nothing of her inner thoughts arched her mouth.

"You confuse me, Lucius Westbrook."

She canted her head. Wisps of hair danced around her face as the wind teased and tormented the tendrils with ever-increasing aggression.

"Are you…?" She trapped her lower lip between her teeth.

Her cheeks turned adorably pink. Regardless, she persevered and pressed on. Clodovea's intrepidness was one of the many facets of her character that beguiled Lucius.

"Are you courting me?"

"I'm sure as the devil trying to."

Heads down against the blustery wind, they angled toward the house, rain pelting them with every rushed step.

"It's not necessary, Lucius. You needn't pretend to be enamored of me."

He wrapped an arm around her waist, drawing her near to protect her from the worst of the wind pummeling them.

Pretending be hanged.

Lucius was polished boots over crisp cravat besotted.

"But what if I want to, sweet dove?"

14

12 March

Hefferwickshire House dining room

Luncheon

Clodovea smiled as the footman placed a selection of scrumptious-looking, triangular-shaped sandwiches before her. She enjoyed her new, slimmer figure—although she'd never be considered willowy or lithe with her generous curves. Nevertheless, that didn't mean she couldn't appreciate an artfully presented plate of bread, cold meats, and cheeses.

Long mid-morning walks and almost daily horseback rides had become her habit and invigorated her appetite. Lifting her knife and fork, she cut the corner off a cucumber sandwich.

Across the table spread with a delicate lace tablecloth, Lucius watched her.

She felt his caressing gaze slide over her hair, down

her shoulders to her hands before skimming upward and settling on her face. This recent ability to sense when he was in the room and when he affixed his attention on her was quite uncanny.

Thrilling and disconcerting.

Maintaining a neutral but pleasant expression, she raised her hesitant gaze to meet his.

He winked as he popped a whole triangle into his mouth and chewed happily.

Clodovea smiled despite herself.

He truly was a charming scamp when he set his mind to it. And he had determined to woo her. His doting behavior these past days had drawn the entire family's attention, and Clodovea had been hard put to pretend she didn't notice the exchanging of speculative and deliberative glances.

She was no nearer to making a decision about marrying Lucius either, but her heart had softened toward him considerably. So much, in truth, that she had to rummage through her memories with a single-minded, resolute focus to scrape up any lingering resentment or anger toward him.

Forgiving him had proved far easier than expected, and it was because this gentler, jovial, considerate Lucius was nearly irresistible. Had those first days of their acquaintance not been hostile and frightening, she strongly suspected she'd be well on her way to loving him.

However, caution and uncertainty still guarded her hesitant heart.

"Let's go to the village this afternoon." Althelia passed her cousin a red satin and silver pickle caster.

"Thank you." Eva helped herself to a pickle before passing the caster to Adolphus. "We can select new ribbons and adornments for your other bonnets, Clodovea."

"A grand idea," her grace agreed, knife poised in the air. "You can also check on the progress of the rest of Clodovea's wardrobe."

"I need to purchase a couple of items myself." A piece of ham dangling from the end of his fork, Adolphus swept the table with his gaze. "Mind if I join you?"

"Not at all. In fact, I'd welcome your company."

Althelia veered her blue-eyed gaze, so like Lucius's, to her other brother. The merest shadow of something unspoken pinched the corners of her eyes. "Yours as well, Lucius."

He dabbed his mouth with his serviette.

Such a well-formed, kissable mouth.

A mouth Clodovea would very much like to taste again.

She dropped her attention to her plate and examined the English Worcester design, lest anyone catch her gaping at him like a moon-eyed *mentecato*—peahead. Taking another bite of her sandwich, she considered the siblings.

Adolphus and Lucius regarded Althelia with affection, and their light-hearted banter reminded Clodovea of her brothers' interactions. Clodovea, however, had always been a bystander—a wistful observer to their comradery—not a participant as Althelia and even Eva were with the Westbrooks.

A familiar pang of sadness nestled near Clodovea's heart.

She'd still had no word from her family—not a

single letter—and enough time had passed that correspondence should've arrived by now. Unless, perhaps, her brothers were exercising extreme caution to avoid putting themselves and her at risk.

She prayed it was the latter, but she wasn't convinced that was the case.

In truth, since her parents' death, she felt a burden to her brothers, particularly Andrés, who would someday be lord of Casa de Vargas as Uncle Gregoria hadn't fathered any sons.

"Why don't I trust that your request is solely because you are eager for my charming company?" Lucius asked, one eyebrow shied high on his forehead. He shook a finger at his sister. "What are you really about?"

Althelia took a sip of tea before giving a delicate shrug. "The Hartigans have opened Lanford Park. Beatty told me this morning. Her sister was called to the house yesterday to resume her duties."

"The devil they have." Adolphus slammed his fist upon the table, rattling the silver utensils and bone china. "They have some nerve, the bloody blighters."

"Language, Adolphus." The Duchess of Latham's admonishment seemed more perfunctory than censorious.

"They were bound to return at some point," the dowager duchess put in as she selected a generous slice of seedcake. "It's been nearly three years since… Well, you know."

She slid an affectionate, protective glance toward Althelia, attending to her meal with particular focus.

The duchess angled her regal, auburn head. "*I do not intend to make them any more welcome now than I did then. As we are the highest-ranking family in the area, I hope others follow our lead.*"

"Now, Margaret." The duke bestowed a benevolent smile upon his wife. "Why don't we wait and see what comes of it? We don't even know which Hartigans are in residence."

Obviously, something had happened between the Hartigans and the Westbrooks.

Tilting her head, Clodovea studied Althelia, picking at her luncheon.

Something most unpleasant, she'd vow, and which involved Althelia.

Taut lines bracketing her mouth and ire sparking in her pretty blue eyes, Eva laid her hand atop Althelia's on the table.

Althelia responded with a stiff half-smile, and an unspoken message passed between the cousins.

"You mustn't fret over me," she said, plucking a grape from her plate. "I have developed a thick skin and am not the timid mouse I once was. I assure you. I can defend myself. Nevertheless, I shan't deny that I do not relish the prospect of encountering Leticia or Peter Hartigan."

Upper lip curled and nose wrinkled as if a herd of manure-covered hogs wallowed on the dining room's Aubusson carpet, Libby made an unladylike sound and muttered something which sounded like "Vermin."

Lucius speared an apple slice. "Of course, I shall accompany you. I have shopping to do too."

Althelia's grateful smile didn't quite reach her eyes.

"I think it wise for Adolphus and Lucius to accompany the girls." His grace directed his attention to his plate before pinning each son with a stay-out-of-trouble look. "But conduct yourselves in a manner worthy of the Westbrook name."

Loud footsteps echoed in the corridor, drawing everyone's attention.

"What in heaven's name?" The duchess trained a disapproving look upon the entrance, which transformed into joy when two men tromped through the opening.

"Surprise, Mama. Papa."

A tall man with jet-black hair and a cocky grin strode into the room. He greatly resembled Adolphus and Lucius, unlike the other man, possessing wavy chestnut locks, bottle-green eyes, and a much more serious expression.

"Leonidas! Fletcher!" her grace cried, rising to embrace her sons. "We had no idea you intended to pay us a visit."

"Yes, well, Fletcher and I didn't exactly plan to do so either." Leonidas's vague response caused every eyebrow in the room to raise except Clodovea's. "But that's a discussion for another time. I'm famished, and I'm sure Fletcher is too."

"Speaking of unexpected guests, what are you

doing at Hefferwickshire, Lucius?" Fletcher's keen gaze flickered back and forth between Lucius and Clodovea.

"I've resigned my position." Lucius's bland stare dared them to probe further. "Thought I might oversee one of Father's estates or try my hand at private investigation."

He'd be an excellent detective.

"Indeed?" Leonidas's seemingly benign question promised he'd interrogate his older brother later.

This family knew each other well, and Lucius's nonchalant response did nothing to dissuade his brothers' probing gazes.

Fletcher scratched his cheek. "I'll wager there's a story behind that decision."

"You'd be right." The dowager chuckled to herself, her eyes full of mischief behind her spectacles. She gave Clodovea a conspiratorial wink.

Oh, *that* wouldn't cause any speculation, as if there weren't enough buzzing about already.

"Sit down, you rapscallions," the dowager ordered, "so we can finish our meal without craning our necks."

"Simms asked me to pass the post along to you."

Leonidas laid a stack of correspondence beside his father's plate. "He apologizes, but there was a disturbance regarding chickens loose in the kitchen he had to remedy."

"*Chickens*? Kitchen?" The Duchess of Latham sent an astonished glance toward the servant's entrance into the dining room. "I don't think I even want to know."

After the newcomers greeted the rest of their family with appropriate kisses on cheeks or firm handshakes, their inquisitive attention rested on Clodovea as they settled into the scarlet and gold striped seats of their respective chairs

Footmen appeared with generously laden plates and placed them before the brothers.

If Clodovea recalled correctly, Fletcher was one of the duchess's sons by her first marriage, whom the Duke of Latham had adopted.

"Brothers, allow me to introduce our houseguest, Clodovea de Soverosa."

Lucius swiftly made the rest of the introductions as the duke distributed several correspondences to the others.

At once Eva tore into her short pile of letters. She laughed out loud. "Laine is coming to England this summer."

"Excellent." The duke nodded. "It's been too long since we saw your brother."

Her grace thumbed through her correspondence before setting all but one aside. After a swift perusual, she announced, "Cousin Cortland Marlow-Westbrook and his family would like to visit in June for a fortnight."

Clodovea had no idea where this particular cousin might be perched on the extensive Westbrook family tree.

Libby, Lucius, and Clodovea also received a letter.

At last.

Her heart thudding unnaturally hard in her chest, Clodovea held the long-awaited missive in both hands. She'd hoped that all her brothers would write and Lupita too. Again, she reassured herself that an overabundance of caution had kept everyone from writing.

Nothing more nefarious.

Turning the letter over, Clodovea stared at the return address, and her meal curdled in her stomach.

Gregoria de Soverosa, lord of Casa de Vargas.

15

Still in Hefferwickshire House's dining room
A few excruciatingly slow tick-tocks of the longcase clock later

A letter from Uncle Gregoria.
Not Andrés or Fernández or Enríquez or even Lupita.

Every instinct Clodovea possessed shouted that the official stationery wouldn't contain good news.

She swallowed, then cleared her throat, unable to meet Lucius's eyes. He'd know how distraught she was, and she refused to come undone in front of him and his family before she'd read her uncle's letter.

After all, she might be mistaken.

Mightn't she?

Clutching the letter to her middle, she rose. "Please excuse me."

This letter was best read alone, for Clodovea

suspected that which she had dreaded was upon her.

"Of course, my dear." Kindness and concern etched a fine line between the duchess's eyebrows. Her keen gaze dropped to the rectangle Clodovea held in a death grip. "Do let us know if you need anything or if we can help in any way."

Offering a tremulous smile, Clodovea swept from the room, nearly running down the corridor. She mouthed a silent, beseeching prayer as she hastened along the passageway, her slippers and skirts making a whooshing sound.

Please don't let it be so.

Please don't let it be so.

She swerved into the drawing room, impatient to know the letter's contents and unwilling to wait until she'd made it to her bedchamber to tear it open.

A well-tended fire crackled and popped behind a gilded screen, warming the room. Winter's chill lingered despite a few intrepid sunbeams caressing the damp, dark brown earth.

Even though Clodovea wore a long-sleeved gown, she tugged the ivory woolen shawl she'd borrowed from

Althelia higher. She still hadn't become accustomed to England's much cooler climate.

Would she ever?

Hurrying to the far window for reading light, she cracked the green wax stamped with Uncle Gregoria's seal with her thumbnail.

She paused, holding the letter in trembling hands, afraid to read the contents.

Get on with it. Stalling will avail you nothing.

Inhaling a bracing breath to prepare herself for the worst, Clodovea skimmed the letter.

An involuntary gasp ripped from her throat, and she pressed a palm against the window frame as dizziness engulfed her. She'd naively believed she'd prepared herself for any eventuality.

She'd been wrong.

So very, very wrong.

Slowly, unable to believe what she'd read, her mind whirling with the appalling accusations, she reread the short, terse letter.

Phrases jumped out at Clodovea, each impacting her with the force of a slap as she struggled to focus through the moisture pooling in her eyes.

You've disgraced the de Soverosa name.
...Caused my good friend Ambassador Tur de Montis undeserved shame and humiliation.

Ambassador Tur de Montis was Uncle Gregoria's friend?

She shut her eyes against what that implicated.

...not welcome any longer.
...forbidden contact with your brothers.
Arranged for a convent...

No. No.
I shan't. I shan't agree.

A cry of dismay ripped from her throat as she clasped a hand over her mouth, the letter fluttering to the floor.

Clodovea squeezed her eyes shut against the despair clawing at her heart and ripping at her mind. She tried to calm her erratic breathing, but the harder she tried to regain her composure, the tighter her lungs cramped.

Banished. Exiled.

Prohibited from contacting her brothers.

Had Andrés and the others agreed to Uncle Gregoria's dictates?

Had they also betrayed her?

Did her brothers blame her as well?

"Clodovea? What is it?"

Lucius.

Engrossed in her frantic, pensive ruminations, Clodovea hadn't heard him enter the drawing room.

She ought to rail at him.

Hit him.

Lay this catastrophe squarely at his feet.

He had caused this debacle.

Instead, she opened her eyes, her mind spinning in shock and grief.

Concern and something more powerful contorted his features and shone in his eyes.

"What has happened, darling?"

Only he could offer her the solace she so desperately craved.

"I've been banished, Lucius."

Still reeling from shock, her world tipped topsy-turvy, Clodovea sucked in a ragged breath, barely able to form the words.

"I'm forbidden to see my brothers. It seems my uncle is close friends with Ambassador Tur de Montis, and he is livid. He blames me for my brothers' expulsion and the ambassador's disgrace. The only recourse he offered is for me to enter an isolated *convento* and…"

Clodovea gasped against the pain shredding her heart and hopes.

"Remain cloistered there for the remainder of my life," she ended on a rasping whisper.

"Buggar that fustian rubbish to hell and back!"

Thunder exploded across Lucius's countenance, and his eyebrows snapped together with such ferocity she nearly heard the crack. Wearing all black except for his cravat's pristine waterfall, he might've been Lucifer himself standing there, straight from Hades, and prepared to exact his wrath upon Uncle Gregoria.

"I shall never let that happen, Clodovea. Never."

He swept her into his arms and carried her to the settee as if she weighed no more than a small child. Only

Lucius made her feel feminine rather than a maladroit, lumpy dumpling. He cradled her in his arms as she wept, heartbroken and hopeless, against his shoulder.

"I'm sorry, my darling." Lucius caressed her back and shoulders, pressing tender kisses into her hair. "I'm so very sorry. Forgive me for causing you this pain. I would cut off my leg rather than see you suffer, sweet dove."

He murmured affectionate promises and assurances as she sobbed.

Clodovea was adrift.

No home. No family.

She was alone.

At last, her reservoir of tears ran dry, and she accepted the handkerchief Lucius pressed into her hand but didn't lift her head from his broad, comforting, and very damp shoulder.

Dabbing at her wet face, she considered her options.

She had only one viable choice.

A shudder rippled through her.

Clodovea raised her head until her eyes met his.

The tenderness there encouraged her—prodded her to say the words.

Yes, she'd made the right decision.

"I'll marry you, Lucius, if you will still have me."

"*If?* Yes, my darling." He broke into a jubilant grin and tightened his embrace. "I don't deserve such a treasure. But I vow before you and the Almighty that I shall spend every minute of every day making amends for the hurt I've caused you."

Clodovea managed a weak smile. "No need to be overly dramatic. I have no great expectations from our union."

Even so, such a match was preferable to what amounted to incarceration.

His chuckle rumbling deep in his chest beneath her cheek caused a genuine smile to frame her mouth.

"I received notice today that my resignation was accepted. It saved the agency from reprimanding me, which likely would've been my dismissal, in any event." He gave her a cockeyed smile. "I am free to marry tomorrow, if you wish."

"*Ahem.*" A male cleared his throat.

Lifting her head, Clodovea peered toward the entrance.

The duke and duchess hovered there, concern written on their faces.

"I presume you received unwelcome news, Clodovea?" The duchess glided into the room, compassion in her eyes.

"I did."

Devasting, life-altering news.

There was no point in denying it or pretending otherwise.

And there was no going back to the life Clodovea had just a few short weeks ago. She'd just agreed to marry Lucius.

Lucius eased her off his lap and then stood, extending a hand to assist her. He brushed a lingering tear from Clodovea's cheek with a bent knuckle before taking her hand and facing his parents.

"We are to wed as soon as possible. I already have a special license."

Clodovea didn't know how he'd managed that when she'd not agreed to marry him until this very moment, but what did it matter?

A smile wreathed the Duke of Latham's face as he advanced into the drawing room, and the duchess's gaze turned misty.

"I do so love weddings," she said with a watery smile.

"I am delighted you shall be joining our family, Clodovea." The duke kissed her cheek. "I suspected you'd snared my son's heart."

Clodovea couldn't bring herself to contradict his grace.

His wife pulled her into a fragrant embrace.

"I am equally thrilled, my dear. I hope you will be very happy."

"Thank you."

What else did one say?

Your son mistook me for a spy, abducted me, and brought me here when he learned his mistake, but it was too late? With no means of my own, if I don't marry him, I'll have to enter a convent?

Somehow—God help her—Clodovea must make this arranged marriage work.

"How soon do you want to marry?" her grace asked.

Clodovea glanced up at Lucius. "I don't know."

"In a fortnight?" His gaze searched hers. "With just those of us at Hefferwickshire attending?"

He gave her the choice, and her heart unfurled at his consideration.

Mayhap this could work.

"*Sí.*"

His family would be present—hers would not.

What would Uncle Gregoria do when he learned she'd outmaneuvered him?

There was nothing he could do, the miserable tyrant.

The Duke of Latham outranked her uncle, and as his daughter-in-law, she would be under his grace's protection. Not just his but Lucius's.

Clodovea swallowed the anxiety constricting her throat.

She'd made her choice and would not entertain regrets or second thoughts. She would be a good wife to Lucius. The past was in the past, and she could not change it. However, Clodovea could face her future with optimism and hope.

Less than a month ago, she'd never have considered Lucius's offer.

Now marriage to him was the only thing that would spare her a fate worse than death.

16

Hefferwickshire stables
A week later
19 March 1826

Where is she?

Lucius drummed his fingertips against his thigh as he inspected the stable's interior.

Where was Clodovea?

She'd sent him a note asking him to meet her in the stables, but his betrothed wasn't here, and it wasn't like her to be late.

Outside, a crow cawed, answered immediately by another—possibly its mate. The bright, cold day portended an early spring, and songbirds lifted their voices in celebration.

Queer how his heart skipped a bit and his stomach felt squishy when he thought of Clodovea as his future wife. Lucius had no regrets about putting aside his career as an agent to start a life with her. And, of more significance, no guilt that he had fallen in love with her.

Francesca had been the love of his youth and had they married, Lucius didn't doubt they would've been content. There would always be a special place in his heart for the love he'd lost.

However, this all-consuming, permeating love for Clodovea...?

It was beyond anything he'd ever experienced—exceeded any love he'd ever imagined. She was part of him, and he of her. Something within Lucius must've recognized that veiled truth when she stumbled into the ambassador's office.

He'd mistaken his powerful and instantaneous reaction as hatred and fury toward his nemesis. Even then, the potent, illogical attraction had baffled him. Infuriated and frustrated too. Theirs was a scintillating meshing of souls, and he prayed every day would be a joyous journey with her.

Lucius had meant every word he'd vowed about making her happy.

Whatever happened, whatever trials and triumphs

awaited *his* Westbrook bride, Lucius would be at her side.

Clodovea mightn't love him the way he adored her, but he hadn't despaired yet.

Mother and Father hadn't loved each other when they'd wed.

Now look at them.

More than once, their public displays of affection had caused their children to blush and squirm in embarrassment. He should like to cause his offspring the same discomfit.

Even after all these years, his parents only had eyes for each other.

Grandmama and Grandfather's arranged marriage had also turned into a love affair. *Le beau monde* still whispered behind hands and fans of their scandalous interludes.

Uncertainty tried to poke her gnarly troll's head into Lucius's pleasant musings.

True, but look what happened to Lucius's other adopted brother, Layton. His wife, Virginia, had run off with another soldier, leaving Layton embittered and cynical.

With a firm shake of his head, Lucius dispelled his misgivings.

Clodovea was nothing like Layton's capricious and unfaithful wife.

He scanned the stable's orderly interior, his nostrils flaring at hay, horses, liniment, and grain aromas—comforting scents from his childhood.

One of the stable hands called to another in the corral, and a calico barn cat padded forward. Purring, she rubbed against his legs before meandering over to lie in a hay pile and groom herself.

A horse snorted, and another answered with a soft whicker.

The cat yawned and pranced from the barn with a disdainful twitch of her mottled orange, black, and gray tail.

Low murmuring in the last stall drew his attention, and Lucius approached the enclosure.

"Ah, there you are."

He rested a forearm atop the stall door.

Clodovea glanced over her shoulder as she stroked a blond-maned sorrel's neck. "She's pregnant, yes?"

Indeed, the mare was very pregnant.

"She is. I believe Father said she is due in May."

A soft smile curved Clodovea's mouth. "Before my parents died, we had several horses in our stables."

Lucius hesitated but then dared to ask, "What happened to your parents?"

She paused in caressing the mare, grief shadowing her pretty profile before she began petting the horse once more. "A fire broke out at a fiesta hosted by my uncle. Several guests died in the crush to escape the *mansion*. Others became trapped inside. My younger brothers were at university, and I was too young to attend. Andrés, my eldest brother, was in another city at the time."

"I'm sorry." How hard it must've been for her, the youngest child and only girl.

Expression pensive, Clodovea gave a little shrug.

"It was ten years ago. I do miss them still." She smoothed a hand over the mare's distended belly. "I was seven when I first saw an *el potro*? *La potra*?—" She scrunched her nose. "What is the English word?"

"Foal?" Lucius offered.

"*Sí*. A foal born." She kissed the mare's neck. "I have—had—a beautiful mare in Spain."

Lucius would see that she had her own horse again. "We'll get you a mount of your choosing."

He couldn't tell if the half-smile she sent him was gratitude or apathy.

"Why did you want to meet me in the stables, Clodovea?"

"I arranged a picnic for us."

A shy smile framed her mouth.

"I thought perhaps you could show me more of Hefferwickshire, and we might find a pretty place to eat. The basket is on the table over there."

She pointed across the way.

Glancing over his shoulder, Lucius spied the hamper on a narrow table beside a lamp and various equine grooming tools.

Three horses regarded him with bored contentment in their respective stalls.

The stable hands would release them into the

paddock for exercise soon.

Lucius grinned and nodded.

"I would like that very much."

Hope that she felt something for him grew.

Why would Clodovea plan such an intimate outing if she didn't harbor a warm sentiment toward him?

She'd been quiet and reserved during their excursion to the village last week, but several times he'd caught her regarding him from beneath her eyelashes. Thankfully, no one had encountered a Hartigan. After a little delicate questioning of the locals, Lucius discovered that only Peter Hartigan had returned to Lanford Park to recuperate. However, no one knew from what. Or if they knew, they weren't willing to share.

Exquisite in a new ruby-red riding habit accented with black velvet they'd collected from the seamstress that day, Clodovea's exotic beauty bludgeoned Lucius.

The women who'd teased Clodovea in London must've frothed with envy.

She was an incomparable.

Ebony ribbons trailed down her back from the

jaunty crimson and black hat angled atop her head. Eyes aglow with wonder, she quite took his breath away.

"Clodovea, has anyone ever told you how beautiful you are?"

Her startled glance and the tell-tale blush sweeping her porcelain cheeks spoke for her.

"There's no need for false flattery, Lucius."

She glanced downward at her breasts and rounded hips and brushed a bit of straw off her skirt.

"I know I'm not fashionable with my dark coloring, full figure, and Spanish accent."

She still didn't perceive her loveliness or know that the lushness of her figure kept him awake at night in anticipation of consummating their vows.

For this would not be a marriage in name only.

Clodovea might not be ready to be his wife in every way right now, but Lucius was confident from her kisses and surreptitious glances that she would be.

In time.

Pray to God it would be soon, or he'd be swimming in the frigid pond at Glenwood Knoll—the small three-acre estate Father had given him outside of Manchester upon learning he'd resigned his post—with such frequency people would remark on his prune-like skin.

"*Fashionable?*" Lucius opened the door and then stepped inside. "What does fashion have to do with anything?"

She pulled a face before kissing the mare's muzzle.

"You know what I mean. I'm an undesirable. A wallflower."

He did know, and it was far past time Clodovea was disabused of the lies she believed about herself.

He placed his palms on the rough wall on either side of her, effectively pinning her in place.

"Lucius, what are you doing?"

Wide-eyed, she shot a glance at either arm, then locked her doe-eyed gaze on his.

"Enlightening you, my love."

Her eyes rounded impossibly more, and she was so winsome and adorable that he couldn't help but drop a kiss on her pert mouth.

"Seldom have I beheld such exquisiteness, Clodovea. And as for your figure…"

He gave her a roguish grin as he pulled her into his

embrace, skimming his hands over her ribs and lower until they rested on the tempting swell of her hips.

"I assure you, my dove, your luscious curves are precisely what every man dreams of."

Pulling her closer until their thighs touched, he nuzzled her ear.

Pupils dilating, she gasped and clutched his shoulders.

Primal male satisfaction thrummed through him.

Excellent.

Most excellent, indeed.

"I eagerly anticipate making you mine in every way once we are married."

Licking her lower lip in consternation, Clodovea averted her gaze briefly before boldly meeting his once more.

She possessed more courage than she realized.

"It doesn't bother you that I'm not willowy? Or fair? Or an Englishwoman?"

Her accent thickening with desire and confusion, she swiped a curl off her cheek.

"That my accent is so obvious?"

"Darling, those among a hundred—no, a thousand—other things are precisely why I love you."

Lucius hadn't meant to tell her yet, but the words tumbled forth of their own accord. And, by Jupiter, he was glad of it.

The secret he had harbored these recent days was out. He wanted the world to know that he, Lucius Westbrook, loved, adored, cherished, and revered Clodovea de Soverosa. Moreover, he didn't care if anyone thought him a jingle-brained, smitten fool.

Clodovea went perfectly still, her berry-red mouth slightly parted.

Was that incredulity or hope shining in her black-lashed eyes? The tiny gold flecks in her irises sparkled as she gazed up at him.

"How can you love me?"

Did she think herself unlovable?

Or did she ask because she couldn't conceive their marriage was anything other than an inconvenient solution to an intolerable situation?

Framing her delicate jaw between his thumb and forefinger, Lucius tilted her face upward.

"Because, Clodovea de Soverosa, as cliché as it sounds, you have stolen my heart, and I am a willing slave to my love for you."

He grinned at her astonished expression.

"*You* love me?" A tiny smile crept the corners of her mouth upward, growing until her face radiated happiness. "You *love* me."

She said it again as if she couldn't believe it.

"You love *me*."

"I do. I love you, my heart. My everything." Staring into her wonderstruck eyes, he kissed her fingers. "And I *want* to marry you."

"I never considered…" Clodovea shook her head. "It's all so overwhelming and unexpected."

"I know." Lucius drew her into his arms again, tucking her head beneath his chin. "And I don't expect you to love me. My love shall be enough for both of us."

For now.

A gratified smile slanted his mouth upward when she wrapped her arms around his waist.

How could something so simple bring such contentment?

Such repletion?

"I do care for you, Lucius, but I don't know if what I feel is love." She sighed and nestled closer. "So much has happened these past weeks. I'm still trying to sort out my emotions. I'm sorry."

The mare shifted and gave him an imperious how-long-do-you-intend-to-intrude-upon-me look.

"Shh." Lucius kissed Clodovea's temple.

"It's I who is sorry, Clodovea, for all that transpired before. Nevertheless, I cannot regret the circumstances that brought you into my life, or else we might never have met."

"Exactly so." Angling her head upward, she touched his scar with a fingertip, then rose onto her toes and placed her lips upon the puckered flesh.

Tears burned behind Lucius's eyes.

She'd never shown any repulsion or disgust regarding his disfigurement.

This one-of-a-kind woman with a large and forgiving heart bestowing such tenderness nearly eviscerated him.

"I shall miss my brothers, of course. And England

is colder than I'm accustomed to, but I shall adjust. *Sí?* Already my English is better."

Clodovea cupped his face with her hand, and he pressed a reverent kiss into her palm.

"For you, Lucius, I shall truly try."

His heart soared to the heavens before he lowered his mouth to hers and tasted the addicting honeyed sweetness.

A rider galloping to a halt outside the stables yanked Lucius back to the present.

"I'll water and brush him, sir."

"Thank you, lad."

Philby?

Lucius poked his head over the stall door.

Sure enough, the stable doors framed Philby's enormous silhouette.

"Come, Clodovea." Lucius took her hand. "Philby wouldn't be here if it weren't important."

A worried expression skittered across her face.

Lucius couldn't reassure her Philby's arrival didn't herald something significant.

As he escorted Clodovea toward the stable's entrance, he waved. "Ho, Philby."

"Westbrook." Philby nodded as his attention slid to Clodovea.

Only someone trained in reading people would've noticed the slightest flare of Philby's eyes and nostrils at Clodovea's transformation.

He sketched a shallow bow.

"Miss de Soverosa. You are looking well."

"Thank you, Señor Philby."

"I'm surprised to see you." Lucius sent a pointed glance to the leather pouch slung over Philby's massive shoulder.

"I have important news for you and Miss de Soverosa."

Nothing in his tone or countenance revealed what that news might be—good or bad.

Lucius glanced down at Clodovea. The private interlude he'd envisioned beneath the oak copse would have to wait.

"I'm afraid we must postpone our picnic."

She raised a shoulder.

"There's always tomorrow. I'll just fetch the hamper." She turned toward the interior.

He touched her arm. "Would you mind if the stable hands enjoy it instead?"

"That's a wonderful idea." A smile wreathed her face.

Philby looked quite envious. "I wouldn't mind a bite myself."

"We'll get you fed, my friend." Grinning, Lucius motioned for Sean Wakeman, one of the stable hands.

"My betrothed had a picnic prepared, but we must postpone our outing. You, Tobie, and the other lads are welcome to enjoy the contents. Please return the basket to the house when you have finished."

"Yes, sir." Sean bobbed his head excitedly before dashing off to tell the other two hands.

"Betrothed?" Philby's eyebrows wrestled with his hairline. His focus wavered between Lucius and Clodovea. Back and forth. Back and forth. "You are affianced, in truth?"

Lucius glanced at Clodovea, unable and unwilling to hide his adoration.

"Yes. Clodovea has honored me by agreeing to become my wife."

The reasons for her acquiescence needn't be mentioned.

"Truth be told, I'm not completely surprised." Philby shook his head, something akin to approval crinkling the corners of his eyes. "She had you at sixes and sevens from the beginning. Bernard, Hancock, Worsley, we all saw it."

Yes. Yes. She did.

Philby grinned, a rare occurrence for the behemoth. "Felicitations to you both."

"Thank you." A becoming flush tinted Clodovea's cheeks.

"When does the happy event occur?"

"Next week." Seven more days and Clodovea would be Mrs. Lucius Westbrook.

Peering past Lucius into the pasture, Philby scratched his jaw. "I presume that means you've resigned?"

He veered his keen regard back to Lucius.

"I have." Lucius would miss the men who had become like brothers to him, but a future with Clodovea was what he wanted now. "Come, let's go to the house, and you can tell us what brings you to Hefferwickshire."

"I have letters from Miss de Soverosa's family, smuggled out of Spain." He gave a cautious glance around and, in a muted voice, murmured, "And news about the former ambassador."

17

Hefferwickshire House
Clodovea's bedchamber
Five hours later

I can leave. Go home. See my family.
Clodovea leaned her head against the cool windowpane as she gazed out the window.

Is that what I still want?

She'd been so homesick for Spain, had yearned to see her brothers and Lupita, but now she dreaded leaving England.

No, she dreaded saying goodbye to Lucius.

Her breath against the cold glass created a small patch of fog.

Her room overlooked verdant meadows, dolloped with fluffy white sheep and sweet-faced cows the color of *café con leche* that Lucius told her were a breed called Guernsey. Soon adorable calves would play in the pastures.

Yesterday, she'd appreciated the bucolic view.

Today, it brought tears of regret to her eyes.

Was it just a week ago a letter had crushed her heart, and today's correspondence infused her first with relief and joy and then even greater despondency than Uncle Gregoria's curt note?

Señor Philby had delivered letters from Lupita and all her brothers.

In defiance of Uncle Gregoria's dictates, they'd managed to pass letters on to Philby.

Lupita might be credited with that cleverness and a newly acquired limp that required a cane.

According to Philby, Lupita had rolled the letters into cylinders and hidden them inside the walking cane. A very special cane indeed.

The rest was a carefully plotted and enacted scheme.

A simple outing to the market that wouldn't raise suspicion.

An absent-minded leaning of the accessory against a stall as Lupita examined produce beneath an awning. After all, how could she properly scrutinize tomatoes with just one hand?

A man with a cane casually perused the same fruits and vegetables and then wandered away, taking Lupita's cane and leaving his behind.

Simple but effective, and as a result, Clodovea had the chance to resume her former life.

In Spain.

She skimmed her gaze over the landscape.

A pair of lambs frolicked in the closest meadow, kicking their little black heels in the air.

Heavily pregnant cows ambled from one grassy spot to another, grazing on the vegetation.

Green.

England was so green compared to Spain.

Clodovea would miss this lush landscape more than she'd have ever believed.

Heaving a sigh, she turned away from the pastoral scenery.

Should she pack her new clothes?

The garments were designed for England's weather, not Spain's warmer clime.

Why wasn't she overjoyed at the prospect of going home?

Ecstatic to see her brothers and Lupita?

Not only had Ambassador Domingo Felix Tur de Montis and several of his cronies been arrested in Spain for treason and causing conflict between the Spanish and English Crowns, but Uncle Gregoria had also suffered an apoplexy and wasn't long for this world.

Andrés would soon be the new lord of Casa de Vargas.

He asked Clodovea to come home posthaste.

He'd even sent money for her journey.

He and her other brothers weren't allowed to return to England quite yet.

Nevertheless, Andrés was hopeful that when everything was said and done, when he'd presented evidence that neither he nor Fernández or Enríquez had any involvement with the ambassador's traitorous plans, they would be exonerated.

However, that would take time. Months perhaps.

Once Clodovea reentered Spain, she mightn't ever be permitted in England again—at least not until her family was acquitted.

As Lucius's wife, immunity would be extended to her.

He'd received a letter today revealing that welcome information as well as a fabricated tale about how she'd left her fan and feathers in the ladies' retiring room where she'd gone to tidy her coiffure. Supposedly, Clodovea had fled the waspish tongues and cruel taunts of the ambassador's mistress and her closest compatriots, leaving her possessions behind. And then the jealous mistress had planted Clodovea's possessions in his office for spite after a tryst with the married ambassador.

The story was flimsy at best.

However, Lucius assured her that people were always willing to believe the worst of others. As Ambassador Tur de Montis *had* been having an affair, there was enough truth to the tale to cause doubt and suspicion.

Every obstacle that prevented Clodovea from returning to Spain no longer existed.

Her uncle's decree that she must enter a convent if she returned to Spain was moot. The need for her and Lucius to marry no longer existed.

Why did that cause an excruciating, searing pain in her heart?

Was this love?

This indiscernible yearning to be with him even when it made no sense?

They should be enemies.

At the very least, she should despise him.

Instead, his heated glances and rakish smiles thrilled her. Had her lying awake at night, staring up at the crimson, pleated canopy above her black walnut baroque four-poster bed and imagining what it would be like to be Lucius's wife.

In every way.

To feel his hands upon her when they made love.

To bear his children.

She put a fist to her mouth to stop the involuntary denial that tried to burst forth.

Clodovea did love Lucius.

This topsy-turvy feeling in her middle and giddiness whenever she saw him.

That was love.

Lucius loved her, and she loved him.

When all else was stripped away, one thing remained.

A burning, all-encompassing desire to be with him. Forever and always.

She brushed happy tears from her cheeks with her fingertips. Hugging herself, she spun in a little circle, her cerulean blue and Brussels lace belling out about her ankles.

A soft wrap on her door interrupted her reverie.

"Come in."

Probably Althelia and Eva offering to help her pack.

Lucius slipped inside, closing the door softly behind him.

It took all her self-control not to hurtle across the room and fling herself into his arms.

Sweeping his gaze around the bedchamber, he combed his hand through his hair, his expression bleak.

Lost. Defeated. Desolate.

Exactly the same emotions swirling inside her.

"I expected you to have begun packing."

"No. I..."

Clodovea shook her head and bit her lower lip.

Would she let pride keep her silent?

She'd been afforded the love of a lifetime—something many people were denied.

So what if England was cold and damp?

Lucius would keep her dry and warm.

So what if she didn't speak English well?

The language of love was all she needed to communicate with him.

What did it matter if she had dark brown hair and hazel eyes and would never be slender?

Lucius desired her just the way she was.

"I don't want to go, Lucius."

Anguish pulled each whispered syllable from her.

Dragging her gaze to meet his, blinking back the sudden rush of unshed tears, she shook her head.

"I don't want to leave you."

"Oh, thank God."

In a blink, Lucius closed the distance between them and hauled her into his embrace. Between the kisses he rained upon her face and head, he murmured brokenly, "I thought you were lost to me. I did not know how I would face a single day without you in it, sweetheart."

"I feel the same." Clodovea touched his face with

her fingertips, loving how the pads scraped across the fine bristle. "It was only when I thought I would never see you again that the truth hit me."

She smiled into his blue, blue eyes. Eyes she wanted to look into first thing upon waking every morning and the last thing she wanted to see before drifting to sleep. Eyes she hoped at least one of their children would also have.

"I love you, Lucius Westbrook."

His eyes grew misty, and emotion rendered his voice husky when he spoke.

"I don't deserve you, Clodovea. I am honored and humbled by your love."

He kissed her with such adoration that tears welled in her eyes.

"But I vow, I shall treasure the gift, every hour of every day for as long as I live."

"I vow the same, Lucius." She tilted her head, her heart so full of love that she thought it couldn't hold any more without exploding. "Mayhap your mission and our midnight meeting were providential."

"Assuredly." Lucius squeezed her waist. "Shall we

go below and tell the others? My family is quite unsettled to think you might return to Spain. They've also grown to love you."

"In a little while." Clodovea glanced toward the bed before giving him what she hoped was a seductive smile. He was to be her husband next week, after all. "I think I should like to learn more about kissing. It's quite fascinating and very enjoyable."

"Indeed, it is, and I am only too happy to oblige my soon-to-be bride's every wish."

The rest of the Westbrooks were made to fret and worry for five and forty minutes as Clodovea's soon-to-be husband taught her a very thorough lesson.

Epilogue

Glenwood Knoll
Manchester, England
July 1827

Lucius stood in the Spanish salon's entry observing his wife as she peeked out the window and nervously tapped her black slippered foot. He'd commissioned the sunroom as a wedding gift for Clodovea so she wouldn't be homesick for Spain, and it was her favorite place at Glenwood Knoll.

"Come, my little dove. Sit down. I'm sure your family will be here soon."

She pivoted toward him, the swell of her belly almost hidden by the empire lines of her violet gown.

Their child would arrive in the autumn.

Never had Lucius anticipated anything more, except, perhaps, their wedding day.

Pressing her palms to her abdomen, Clodovea

nodded. "I cannot imagine why I'm so anxious."

"Because you are eager to see them. It's been almost a year and a half."

It had taken over a year to clear the de Soverosa name, but with the assistance of several influential people at the Duke of Latham's behest, the matter had finally been resolved. In fact, he meant to surprise her with a trip to Spain next year after the babe was old enough to travel.

Putting an arm around her shoulders, Lucius guided her to the vibrant claret and gold curved arm couch and urged her to sit.

Sinking gracefully onto the cushion despite her pregnancy, Clodovea sighed before lacing her fingers with his as she leaned into his shoulder.

Lucius rested an ankle on his knee and traced a figure-eight across her nape.

This kind of contentment was priceless.

She toyed with the double swan jet cameo pendant he'd given her for her birthday. Unable to recover the pieces of her necklace to restore it, Lucius had the one she now wore custom made.

"How goes your newest case?" she asked, probably to take her mind off her brothers' imminent arrival.

He'd opened his private investigator venture out of a quaint office in Manchester six months ago, and so far, Lucius had no shortage of clients. Privacy prevented him from revealing details of the investigations with Clodovea. However, he did share snippets that wouldn't jeopardize his clients' identities.

On occasion, he consulted his cousin Torrian Westbrook, who'd proved invaluable.

Lucius chuckled and focused on caressing the sensitive spot just below her ear.

Clodovea angled her head to give him better access.

"Let's just say that when I opened the agency, I never imagined I'd be searching for a tropical bird thief."

Eleven birds, including parrots and cockatoos, had gone missing over the past year.

"Hmm. That is odd." Clodovea squinted in concentration. "I'd suspect a traveling show. A fair or circus. Or a collector of rare birds." She tapped her fingers. "Or perhaps someone who owns an aviary."

She made good points. "Excellent suggestions, all."

Beaumans, Glenwood Knoll's butler, appeared in the doorway. "Mrs. Osborne wanted to check that you wish the milk served with the tea and coffee heated."

Clodovea nodded. "Yes, please."

The cook often double-checked that un-British detail.

Beaumans would never say so, but his nostrils flared at the uncivilized notion of tainting tea with *warm* milk, let alone serving coffee—the barbaric beverage—in fine bone china.

"Very good, madam."

The butler disappeared as silently as he'd appeared.

"I think you've offended his delicate sensibilities," Lucius said, staring at the vacant space where the majordomo had stood moments before.

Clodovea giggled. "It's not the first time, nor will it be the last."

"I love it when you laugh." Lucius swept her mouth with his. "In truth, I love everything about you, darling."

Frowning, she eyed her tummy. "Even though I'm

getting as large as a whale?"

"Never say so." Lucius bent and kissed her belly.

"Hello in there. This is your papa. Your mama and I cannot wait to meet you."

He straightened and caught Clodovea's soft-eyed gaze.

"I think he hears you." Her eyes went wide, and a smile arched her mouth. "He's moving. Feel."

She pressed Lucius's hand to her rounded abdomen.

The babe gave a little kick, then two more.

"He cannot wait to meet us either," she said softly.

Lucius caressed her cheek. "How can you be so certain you carry a boy?"

"I honestly don't know." Her expression took on a faraway look. "It's something I feel."

"You know, my love, that it matters not to me whether the babe is a boy or girl?"

Lucius cupped her cheek.

"I know."

The sounds of wheels crunching gravel carried into the salon.

"They're here!" Clodovea pushed to her feet, her face radiant. "I cannot wait for them to meet you."

Lucius wasn't as positive their reception would be as warm as Clodovea anticipated.

He waggled his eyebrows.

"Should I tell them I have more brothers than you do? Just in case they are inclined to violence against my person?"

Had anyone done to Althelia what Lucius had done to Clodovea, he would've pounded them into next month.

She pursed her mouth, though her eyes brimmed with mirth.

"It's not a contest, Lucius."

Yes, but he'd incriminated their sister, abducted her, held her prisoner, and made it impossible for Clodovea to see her family for months.

As if reading his mind, she slipped her hand into his as they faced the entrance together.

"They won't hold a grudge, Lucius. Trust me. Not when they know I love you."

Glancing down, his love for this precious woman

nearly undid him. "I do trust you, my heart. Whatever the future holds, I shall always trust you."

"And I you, my love."

"Let's meet those brothers of yours together, shall we?"

"*Sí.*"

About the Author

USA Today Bestselling author COLLETTE CAMERON® is renowned for her Scottish and Regency historical romance novels featuring daring rogues, scoundrels, and the strong heroines who capture their hearts. Her stories are filled with inspiration and humor, making them the perfect escape for fans of *Sweet-to-Spicy Timeless Romances*®. Living in Oregon, Collette is a confessed chocoholic and dreams of spending part of her time in Scotland. From the rugged highlands to the refined drawing rooms of Regency England, Collette's stories transport you to another time and place, where love and adventure are just a page away.

Explore Collette's worlds at collettecameron.com!

Join her VIP Reader Club and FREE newsletter. Giggles guaranteed!

http://bit.ly/TheRegencyRoseGift

FREE STARTER LIBRARY FOR NEWCOMERS: Subscribers to Collette's The Regency Rose® VIP Reader Club get updates on book releases, cover reveals, contests, and giveaways she reserves exclusively for newsletter subscribers. Also, any deals, sales, or special promotions are offered to club members first.

WESTBROOK FAMILY

Gerhardt Westbrook, 5th Duke of Latham (Deceased)

married to

Elizabeth (Libby) Everson, Dowager Duchess of Latham

Haygarth, Westbrook 6th Duke of Latham married to Margaret Ellison, Duchess of Latham			Edwin	Prentis	Maynard	Connell	Reuban (Mary-Wife)
Children: Adolphus Lucious Leonidas Darius Cassius Althelia Layton (Adopted Son) Fletcher (Adopted Son)			Children: Torrian Edina Asher Drake Chase Kade	Children: Rebecca Abraham Samuel Mathew Bethany Hannah Adam Caleb	Children: Fern Hunter Forest Skyler Luke Slater Cordelia	Children: Cole Kirk Bruce Reed Rowena	Children: Emerson Rogan Eva Laine Clarke Mynna
Gerhardt's brother: Solomon Westbrook 3rd son (Wife Eliza)				Gerhardt's brother: Benedict Westbrook 2nd son (Wife Janet Marlow)			
Charles	Henry	George	Fredrick	Joseph	David	Jane	Robert
Gerhard II	Mariam	George Jr	Simon	Cortland	Lawrence	Mary	Lucy
Caroline	Elizabeth	Martha	Doreen	Oscar	Terrance	Joanne	Ralph
Haygarth II	Judith	Mable	Dorothy		Margo	Sarah	Fulton
		Emma	Timothy		Bessie		Jude
		Priscilla			Hugh		Jonah
					Deborah		

From the Desk of Collette Cameron

Thank you for reading MISSION AT MIDNIGHT and watching Clodovea and Lucius's journey from enemies to lovers. Theirs was a hard-won happily ever after, but aren't those the best kinds?

If you missed how to pronounce Clodovea's name in the novel, it is Clōde–oh-vee. I know it can be a bit of a struggle to pronounce a character's unusual name, but I am confident my readers will adjust, just as they have adjusted to American spelling, punctuation, and grammar in my books.

I left a couple of questions unanswered in MISSION AT MIDNIGHT, including the incident between Althelia and the Hartigans and why Fletcher and Leonidas made an unexpected appearance at Hefferwickshire House. You'll have to read their stories to discover the answers.

If you haven't read the prequel to the Chronicles of the Westbrook Brides series, MIDNIGHT CHRISTMAS WALTZ, you might consider doing so. I give you glimpses of the eight Westbrook siblings, which will help you establish a foundation for the first books in the series.

Lest anyone is concerned about historical accuracy, Ambassador Domingo Felix Tur de Montis and his nefarious activities are completely fabricated. Also, though Clodovea is Spanish, I've only included a few Spanish words and phrases for easy reading.

Adolphus's story, THE MIDNIGHT MARQUESS, is the next book in the series.

To stay abreast of the releases of the other books in the Chronicles of the Westbrook Brides Series or other upcoming releases, you can subscribe to my newsletter (the link is below) or visit my author world at collettecameron.com.

I hope you enjoyed a romantic escape for a few hours with Lucius and Clodovea. If you liked their story, please consider leaving a review. I would appreciate it so very much.

Hugs,

Collette

Connect with Collette!

Check out her author world:
collettecameron.com

Join her Reader Group:
www.facebook.com/groups/CollettesCheris

Subscribe to her newsletter:
signup.collettecameron.com/TheRegencyRoseGift
and receive FREE Books.

Follow Collette!

BookBub: bookbub.com/authors/collette-cameron
Facebook: facebook.com/collettecameronauthor
Instagram: instagram.com/collettecameronauthor
Goodreads: goodreads.com/author/Collette_Cameron

Made in the USA
Monee, IL
18 May 2023